Regina Silsby's Secret War

by Thomas J. Brodeur

JOURNEY
FORTH

Greenville, South Carolina

Library of Congress Cataloging-in-Publication Data
Brodeur, Tom.
  Regina Silsby's secret war / by Thomas J. Brodeur.
      p. cm.
  Summary: The daughter of a wealthy ship owner uses the superstitions of the day to divert the British forces and support the Sons of Liberty following the Boston Tea Party.
  ISBN 1-59166-235-4 (perfect bound pbk. : alk. paper)
  [1. Boston (Mass.) — History — Colonial period, ca. 1600-1775 — Juvenile fiction. 2. Boston (Mass.) — History — Colonial period, ca. 1600-1775 — Fiction. 3. Ghosts — Fiction. 4. Superstition — Fiction. 5. Boston Tea Party, 1773 — Fiction.] I. Title.
  PZ7.B786113Re 2004
  [Fic] — dc22

                                                    2004001319

Design by Brannon McAllister
Cover illustration by Justin Gerard
Composition by Melissa Matos
©2004 BJU Press
Greenville, SC 29614
Printed in the United States of America
All rights reserved
ISBN 1-59166-235-4
15 14 13 12 11 10 9 8 7 6 5 4 3 2 1

To my darling daughter Michelle —
May you always enjoy
the adventure of life
that God has given you

Contents

One

The Tea Party

Rachel Winslow stumbled on a cobblestone. Icy winds billowed through her cloak, almost hurling her headlong.

"Mind your step, Rachel," said Abigail Sutton. "Stay with me in the lamplight."

Rachel bent her back to the wind and wrestled the hood whipping about her face.

"Such a bitter night," she said.

"At least the snows have stopped."

Trees in the King's Chapel cemetery writhed like tormented souls. The houses opposite were dark, their chimneys streaming ribbons of smoke. A black sky of boiling clouds rolled overhead.

Rachel halted.

"For pity's sake," Abigail said, her breath frosting on the wind. "Why are you stopping?"

"I think I have muddied my skirts," Rachel said. She stooped to inspect the fabric blustering about her ankles.

"Get you home and look at them there," Abigail said, "or you'll lose your fingers to frostbite, and then you won't be able to play the organ at Christmas Eve services."

"Fetch your lantern here."

"Are you mad? I'll not go near that graveyard. You've heard the stories. Those wretched corpses will break through the soil and drag us to perdition with them."

Rachel heaved a sigh that iced in front of her. She trudged to Abigail's side.

"Why should we be any safer here in the street?" she said.

"A wicked place, that cemetery," Abigail said, "especially tonight. Every demon in the colony will be cavorting there. 'Tis a wonder they haven't spied us already. Now come along."

"Wait," Rachel said, grabbing Abigail's sleeve. "I haven't yet seen my skirts."

"I shan't tarry here another moment. We'll be carried off to our dooms."

"I'm more fearful of tumbling into the gutter."

Abigail eyed the snowy mounds lining the lane. Animal waste and the muddy wheels of a hundred wagons had reduced them to rutted, filthy mire. She shuddered.

"Let us be off," she said. "One way or another . . . we shall surely catch our deaths."

A bellow paralyzed the girls. From an alley lunged an enormous man, his shoulders wrapped in a ragged blanket. Feathers sprouted from his braided hair. The brute's face was painted black, and with fierce eyes he glared at the girls. A tomahawk quivered in his fist.

Abigail screamed. She dropped the lantern and flung herself into Rachel's arms. The Indian gazed quizzically at the girls, then scooped up Abigail's lamp and returned it to her. Lace cuffs fluttered at his wrists.

"Home, ladies," he said in impeccable English. " 'Tis not a night for young women to be wandering about. Off with you now. Hurry on."

Under his ragged cloak the Indian wore a waistcoat of rich brocade with a watch chain draped across his belly. Silk stockings stretched from the knees of his breeches to a pair of leather shoes with silver buckles. He left the girls staring after him and tramped down the lane. From the alley at his back tumbled an avalanche of screaming savages. Painted warriors poured past the girls waving hatchets, clubs, and staves.

"Good evening, ladies. Begging your pardon," the Indians said as they hurried by. The warriors' frayed shrouds hardly hid the fine woolen cloaks, linen ruffles and silk stockings worn beneath. Brass lanterns bobbed in gloved hands, and hobnailed shoes clattered on the cobbles.

"Peter Slater," Rachel said, recognizing the rope maker's apprentice.

"Rachel," he said, his white eyes popping from his blackened face. "What's got you out and about this night? Come to join in our merriment, I suppose?"

"What merriment?"

"You don't know? All Boston is turning out for it."

"How do you come to be here?" she said. "Hasn't Mr. Gray taken to locking you in your room?"

"Do you think I've learned nothing, being apprenticed to a rope maker as I am? I knotted my bedding together and escaped through the window. Come along to Griffin's Wharf with us. You come too, Abigail."

"Griffin's Wharf?" Abigail said. "It is halfway across town."

" 'Tis but a few streets," he said. "You won't want to miss this. The harbor's to be a tea pot tonight."

"You're talking nonsense," Rachel said, "as usual."

"Not at all. You must come, Rachel. 'Twill be a grand spectacle—something of an early Christmas present for King George."

"Gracious, I shouldn't want to miss that. What say you, Abigail? Let's go see."

"My father will be in fits. Yours too, I daresay."

"We'll only be a minute. Come along."

Peter grabbed Rachel's wrist and dragged her into the mob.

"Rachel," Abigail said, "don't leave me all alone. Rachel!"

She gathered her skirts and ran after them.

"Unhand me, Peter," Rachel said. "I can walk well enough by myself."

"Hush, Rachel, no names."

"Who's to hear me in this bedlam? Peter, you are hurting me."

"Make way, make way," he said, wading through a cascade of savages spilling from the Hound's Tooth Tavern. Others poured from the Old State House. The war parties

4

traded cheers with tailored men and bonneted women bustling along the walkways. Children scampered down the streets tooting fifes and tapping drums. Even dogs loped about baying and barking. Overhead windows flung open, and sleepy inhabitants gazed down on the tumult swirling toward the waterfront.

At Griffin's Wharf a great bonfire blazed. Stuffed effigies of soldiers and king's agents dangled above the crowd. Men and boys were climbing the trees and hanging lanterns in the boughs.

"Citizens of Boston," shouted a red-faced man with a woolen scarf bundled about his ears. "Countrymen! Read here of England's latest assault on our liberties. One penny, one penny."

He waved a pamphlet in Rachel's face.

"One penny, lass," he said. "Every household must see this. One penny, sir. One penny for an account of the king's latest outrages against the American Colonies. I thank you, sir. One penny."

Young men marched about the square singing and chanting verse.

"A wondrous sight," Peter said above the din. "All Boston must be here."

"This is madness," Abigail said. "It is worse than a Pope's Day celebration. Rachel, we shouldn't be here."

"We'll be home soon enough. Peter, what is all this fuss about?"

"The tea ships," he said, pointing along the wharf. "There's the *Dartmouth*, and astern of her are the *Beaver* and the *Eleanor*. The *Eleanor's* mine."

"Yours?"

"We're going to empty them."

"Who?"

"The Sons of Liberty, of course."

"Upon my word," Abigail said. "Are you one of that rabble?"

"Look there," Peter said. A dour Indian chief was leading his war party aboard the *Dartmouth*.

"Stand aside," the chief told the ship's captain.

"I'll not yield," the captain said, "until I have your assurance that my crew will not be harmed."

"No harm crew," said the chief. "Only tea."

The captain accepted his promise, and the chief ordered the ship's crew detained on the quarter deck. Moments later Indian braves were swarming into the *Dartmouth's* hold. With tomahawks they hacked the tea chests apart and dumped their canvas sacks over the rails. Cheers sounded along the wharf.

"Begging your pardon, Miss Rachel, Miss Abigail," Peter said, "but I must pay my respects to the *Eleanor*. You'll watch for me, won't you?"

"Don't be too long about it," Rachel said. "My father shan't look kindly on this."

"He'll never know you were here. As soon as I've done my duty, I'll see you both safely home."

After a hasty bow he scrambled toward the wharf.

"He is mad," Abigail said.

"And all Boston, apparently," Rachel said. "Every gun in the Royal Navy is looking down on us."

She gazed across the harbor where a hundred British warships clogged the waterway. Two-deckers, frigates, sloops, and transports huddled together beneath a forest of masts and spars. Cabin lights shimmered throughout the armada, and many decks were crowded with crewmen watching the commotion ashore.

"One shot would have this entire mob fleeing for their cellars," she said. "I wonder why the fleet doesn't do something."

Her pulse quickened.

"Abigail," she said. "Fort Hill."

"I beg your pardon?"

"Fort Hill and the South Battery are at our back. There must be six regiments of soldiers quartered there. They could easily trap us all in the square."

"Oh, Rachel, 'twill be another Boston Massacre. What shall we do? We could be arrested or even killed."

"Let us be gone at once."

"But Peter . . . he promised to see us home."

"He'll be too long about his present chore, I expect. Come."

She tugged Abigail through the crowd.

"Be on your guard," Rachel said to everyone she passed. "Remember the soldiers at Fort Hill."

"Let them come," shouted a youth. "See if they have the stomach to join our tea party."

"Bring on the redcoats," said another. "We'll show them who owns Boston town."

"Tory," a boy yelled. He hurled a rotten turnip that splattered on Rachel's skirt. Other boys pelted her with stones and clumps of mud. A drunken man, his tricornered hat askew atop his head, grabbed her shoulders with grimy hands.

"You're daft, lass," he said through a toothless sneer. "What's eighty or ninety lobster-backs against the whole of Boston?"

She winced at his odious breath and pried herself from his grip.

"Look at them run," the boys said. "All girls are cowards."

Together Rachel and Abigail fled beneath a hail of rock and rubbish. At Fish Street they paused to catch their breath.

"Lunatics," Rachel said. "Stone and mud will be of little use against muskets."

"Fie on those ruffians," Abigail said. "Just look at my skirts. How shall I explain this to my mother?"

"My dress is hardly better. Follow me."

The girls retraced their steps through the town. At each corner the crowds thinned, until at last the girls were walking empty lanes.

"What's the time?" Abigail said. "We must be an hour past due."

"Heavens," Rachel said. In the halo of a street lamp appeared a cluster of grim figures. Their red coats were crossed by white straps, and tricornered caps of black crowned their heads. Muskets gleamed in the lamplight.

"Seal off that lane yonder," said a sergeant. "Arrest anyone you see."

Abigail shrieked.

"There's a pretty pair," the sergeant said. "Bring them here."

"They are mere women," said another, "not Sons of Liberty."

"I'll wager they're in league with the scoundrels. Arrest them."

Two soldiers tramped toward the girls, bayonets fixed to their muskets.

"Oh, mercy," Abigail said. "We shall never be seen again."

"Let us separate," Rachel said. "They cannot chase the both of us."

Abigail stood petrified.

"Your house is but a block from here," Rachel said. "Go."

A swat to Abigail's rump sent her scooting into the darkness. Rachel fled in the opposite direction. Boots thumped on the pavement at her back. Both soldiers were chasing her.

"You, there," one said. "Halt, in the name of the king."

She dared not. If caught, she would be pilloried, thrown into prison, or worse. Up the hill toward King's Chapel she tumbled in a rush of billowing lace and linen. The soldiers were closing on her. How could she escape them, when every corner was brightened by a lantern?

She pushed through a picket gate and fled into the garden beyond. Moments later the soldiers banged through the same entry, one man cursing as he stumbled over a barrow. By then she was past the carriage house and crossing the street beyond. In a cluster of elm trees she paused to gasp for breath.

"There," said one soldier from across the lane. She fled through the trees to the far alley.

At last, her lungs ballooning and collapsing with each breath, she staggered against the iron fence of the King's

Chapel cemetery. Home and safety were just beyond, but the void separating her from them suddenly seemed ferocious. Was there any truth to the horrible tales people told of skeletons and spirits grasping at ankles, trying to pull trespassers into their graves? All Boston whispered of hapless souls snared by the graveyard's ghouls. Would she become their next victim?

On the other hand, only a raving madman would pursue her there. She lurched through the spiked gate and stumbled into the maze of tombstones. Clumps of snow littered the earth like fallen bodies. The trees above formed a cavern of ice and frost.

Frantically she trampled the graves. If she ran fast enough, she might elude any evil spirits lurking beneath the frozen sod.

"Please, Lord," she prayed, "let not the demons awaken this night."

Her toe struck a stone and she fell, banging her brow on a granite marker. Dazed, she lifted her face from a snow drift and discovered a carved skull and crossed bones leering back at her. The iron gate creaked open. Her pursuers were entering the graveyard.

There was no place to hide. She struggled through a hedge toward a second gate at the back of the chapel. The bushes clawed her cloak from her shoulders. She abandoned the garment and hurled herself against the back gate. It was bolted shut.

"This way," came a brusque voice. The soldiers searched among the graves, prodding shrubs and mounds with their bayonets. Rachel cringed against the iron bars. A frigid blast pierced her dress, chilling her marrow. Her jaw began to vibrate.

"Halt," the first soldier said. "Who goes there?"

He leveled his musket at a dark phantom lurking behind a tombstone. The stranger reeled and staggered as if in great agony.

"Speak," the soldier said. "State your name."

Into the shadows the trespasser wandered. He sank to the ground and cowered in a trembling heap. The soldiers advanced on him.

"Get up, I say," the first soldier demanded. He prodded the quivering lump with his boot.

"Empty," said the second soldier. " 'Tis merely her cloak."

Rachel peered through the hedge and recognized her own cape tangled on a gravestone. The soldiers were stooping to inspect the garment.

"Where did she go?" said the first, glancing about. His companion wiped a layer of frost from the stone.

"Silsby," he read from the granite. "Regina Silsby."

"Look here," said the first. "Fresh footprints. They stop at the grave."

"There's blood on the headstone," his companion said. "And what's this in the snow? It looks like a face."

"So it is. A woman's face."

The two men stared at each other.

" 'Tis a ghost we've been chasing."

"Or a devil straight from hell."

Slowly they retreated from the grave. Dead leaves danced about them on a sudden gust of wind. The trees spilled sheets of snow that swirled through the cemetery like living things.

" 'Twas not to chase spirits I joined the king's regiments," said the first soldier.

A limb cracked. Icy shards rained on the men. The fractured branch groaned in the wind, then snapped off and plummeted to earth. With a yelp the soldiers leapt backward.

"Saints alive," said the first. "We may have been killed."

"I'll not stay another minute in this foul place," said the other. He turned to flee and tumbled backward.

"I'm caught," he shrieked. "She's grabbed me."

His companion was already bounding toward the cemetery gate.

"Help," the fallen soldier said. "Let me go."

His terrified screams filled the graveyard. Finally he freed himself and hobbled away into the darkness, leaving behind his boot. The iron gate groaned on its hinges and banged shut.

Rachel peered across the deserted cemetery. Her cloak was still flapping in the breeze, pinned to the grave by the fallen limb. Cautiously she crept from her hiding place. Despite the chill her blouse was damp with sweat, and her heart was pounding against her ribs. Strands of hair slapped her cheeks. She brushed aside the tousled locks and read the tombstone's inscription:

Here lies ye
body of
Regina Silsby

aged 21
departed this life
Nouem 15, 1742

None but ye heart
knows its sorrow
and none can

The poem's last line was obscured by dead grass and patches of snow. Trembling, Rachel tugged free her cloak and threw it over her shoulders. The soldier's boot lay where he had left it, wedged between a foot stone and a granite slab. She picked her way past the graves and returned to the front gate. Seeing no one in the street, she slipped past the iron bars and fled for the warm, yellow windows of home.

Two

Intruders

"Confound this wig," Jeremiah Winslow said. "Ruined! How could you let the dog at it?"

"Who left it on the reading chair?" Mrs. Winslow said.

Her husband sputtered into silence. He himself had set his hairpiece on the chair's armrest the previous evening. Too many times his wife had chided him for scattering his belongings about the house. Now she was letting him suffer for his untidiness. From the dining room table Winslow watched her arrange evergreen sprigs in a basket on the sideboard. A gown of pale blue flowed from her slender waist to her toes. Woven into the fabric were tiny pink blossoms that matched the blush in her cheeks. She was humming a yuletide tune.

"Next week is the governor's banquet," Winslow said. "How shall I go without my wig?"

"Powder your own hair, I suppose," she said, scratching the stubble that dotted his shaved pate.

"Breakfast," Rachel said. She swept into the room with a basket of steaming muffins. Her dark hair was bundled beneath a lace cap tied behind her neck. Flour dusted the apron shielding her green gown.

"My, but it is cold outside," she said. "I nearly froze to death walking between the well and the house."

"Goodness, child," her father said. "Is that blood on your scalp?"

"I tripped and banged my head last night."

"Have you washed it?" Mrs. Winslow said, inspecting the wound.

"Aye, Mother. 'Twill mend quickly enough. And you, Father! What have you done to your wig?"

"The dog," he said, "seems to have taken a fancy to it."

By the hearth lay the offending hound, mournfully gazing at his master. Winslow scowled at the animal, until his eyes fell on the open Bible before him. Leaping from the page was the proverb "A righteous man regardeth the life of his beast . . ."

Winslow mustered enough compassion to scratch the dog's ear, then leaned back his chair and thrust open the window. Frigid gusts stirred the curtains. He hurled his wig into the snow and watched a goat sniff the headpiece. One of the pigs wandered over and plopped his rump on it. Winslow heaved a sigh and lowered the sash.

"A fortnight's wages lost," he said.

"You always complained that it itched too much," Rachel said.

"I suppose I shall have to purchase a replacement from the wig maker. Rachel, dear, is that plum pudding I smell?"

"Aye, and roast duck and minced kidney pies."

"And," he said, inspecting her soiled apron, "unless I am very much mistaken, apple butter, gooseberry tarts, and apricot preserves."

"Basted with brandy," she said. "We shall sup like royalty this evening."

"Brandy?" said a gravelly voice from the hall. "I'll have a dram of that."

Rachel's grandfather shuffled into the room, his gray locks gathered into a tangled queue at the back of his neck. From his stooped shoulders hung an unbuttoned waistcoat. His breeches were loose at the knee, and one of his shoes was unbuckled. He dropped into a chair and began stuffing tobacco into his pipe.

"Hain't a single tea leaf left on them ships," he said. "Three-hundred-forty chests, all floating in Boston harbor."

"How do you come by this information so quickly, sir?" Winslow said.

"Henry Gibbett told me this morning while I was feeding the chickens. Said he was just coming home after watching the whole tea party from Griffin's Wharf."

"That Samuel Adams rogue is behind this," Winslow said, "and a fat price Boston will pay for such wanton revelry. Tea party, indeed. I put the cost at sixty thousand pounds. All for a few pence worth of tax."

"You should be thanking the good Lord that none of your packet ships were carrying English tea. Where's that brandy?"

"In the apricot preserves," Rachel said. "You'll have to fetch yourself out to the kitchen to get some."

"Bah."

He lit his pipe with a candle from the table.

"Can we not bless the meal," Mrs. Winslow said, "and continue this enchanting conversation as we dine?"

All heads bowed.

"For this repast," Winslow prayed, "we give Thee thanks, most gracious God. Bless us this day, and may all that we do bring honor to Thine holy name. Amen."

"Amen."

"Rachel," Winslow said while buttering a muffin, "how does your reading progress? Why not share with us something from the gospels?"

He passed the open Bible to her. She fanned the pages to the New Testament.

"Master," she read, *"who did sin, this man, or his parents, that he was born blind? Jesus answered, Neither hath this man sinned, nor his parents: but that the works of God should be made manifest in him."*

"A fine choice," Winslow said. "And what's the lesson in it, my dear?"

"There's nothing too hard for the Lord Jesus."

"Aye, but there's more to it than that," he said. "This passage reminds us that even adversity serves a purpose for good. So often God's ways mystify and confuse us. But the Lord works His will in our lives, much as an archer shoots an arrow. First the marksman cradles his choicest missile in his bow, then draws back the cord. His bow resists, but the archer firmly bends the wood to his will. Stretched to its breaking point, the bow quakes and shudders in the master's hand until, at exactly the right moment, the archer lets fly his arrow. Swiftly the missile streaks, invisible, unstoppable, striking straight and true. In God's hands we are like that bow, stretched by hardships and adversities. And God's purpose is like the arrow, unleashed after much strain and struggle, but always at the proper moment. True to its mark God's purpose flies, accomplishing just what the Lord intended. Remember, child: even in affliction, the Almighty is working His ways. And like the archer's arrow, God's purpose will be released in our lives, making its mark for eternity."

Winslow nodded solemnly, satisfied with his sermon.

"Will you be teaching her to shoot arrows?" Grandfather said between puffs. "Muskets are more practical these days."

Winslow scowled at him.

A loud hammering rattled the door. Rachel rose and scurried to the front hall. Through the lace curtain she spied four British officers crowding the front step. At their backs stood a cluster of red-coated soldiers.

Her heart slammed into her throat. The squad's sergeant was the very man who had ordered her chased the previous night. He had found her out and had come to arrest her. Fighting an urge to run, she unlatched the door.

"Good morrow, sirs," she said, her voice wavering as she curtsied.

"What's your name, girl?" said the shortest of the officers. His face was smooth and pale, his lips thin. A black, tricornered hat sat atop an immaculate white wig. Lace ruffles fluttered at his throat, and gold buttons festooned his crimson coat. With long, delicate fingers he gripped an ornate sword that dangled to the toes of his gleaming black boots.

"Blast you, girl," he said. "Answer my question."

"Your servant, sir. I am Rachel Winslow. And you are . . . ?"

"I'll speak to the master of the house," he said, pressing a scented linen to his nose.

"Mr. Winslow is still at breakfast," she said. "If you would care to sit here in the hall until—"

"Do you know who I am?"

"Should I?"

The officer arched an eyebrow. He turned to the sergeant and said, "Are all American girls this brazen?"

"Very nearly, my lord," the sergeant said. "You mind your manners, missy. This here's the son of the Earl of Leicester."

"Inform your father," said the earl's son, "that Captain James Dudley of his majesty's 64th Regiment of Foot would speak with him. And be quick about it, girl."

"At once, my lord," she said, curtsying again. She slipped from the hall to the dining room.

"Father," she said, "soldiers are at the door. Their captain, one James Dudley, wishes a word with you."

"Why should soldiers come to see me?" Winslow said. "I know no Capt. Dudley."

"He is the son of the Earl of Leicester."

"You don't say," he said, bolting from his chair.

"I do say," said the captain. He had followed Rachel to the dining room entry. "Are you the master of this domicile?"

"I am Jeremiah Winslow. My family and I are honored by your presence, my lord."

Mrs. Winslow sat silently. Rachel's grandfather puffed his pipe.

"Col. Leslie has ordered billeting for my men," Dudley said. "I and three of my officers will board here."

"Billeting!" Winslow said.

Dudley snapped his fingers. A musketed soldier tramped into the room, tracking mud on the floor. He drew a parchment from a leather pouch and handed it to the captain.

"After last night's tea party, as you rebels are calling it," Dudley said, "the colonel thinks it best to extend his majesty's presence through the town."

"If you consider me one of those howling savages," Winslow said, "who call themselves Sons of Liberty—"

"A fine house, this," Dudley said, "one of the handsomest in all Boston, I'm told. Ought to board three or four quite comfortably."

"Never in my life," Winslow said, "have I condoned the destruction of private property. Nor do I—"

"I'll post myself and three of my officers here. Bradshaw, Rogers, upstairs with the both of you. Lively now. Sgt. Hodges, take my things to the corner room."

"Impossible," Winslow said. "That is my chamber."

Dudley fingered the silver tea set on the sideboard.

"You're a wealthy man, Winslow," he said. "Shipmaster, are you not?"

"I am the owner of Winslow and Company, aye."

"How many ships have you?"

"Twelve. Four are in port just now."

"A veritable fleet," Dudley said. "So, what is it you're smuggling, man? Rum? Molasses? Slaves?"

"I am an honest tradesman."

"There's no such thing in Boston."

"Capt. Dudley, I must protest. You've no right to—"

"I am a captain in his majesty's regiments, and an earl's son besides," Dudley said. "I've a right to do anything I please, even to clapping irons on you."

"My lord, there are many Bostonians who still revere their king."

"If that be so, the king's loyal subjects will hardly object to hosting his majesty's humble servants on their premises. Will they, Winslow?"

"My family's fealty to the crown has never been questioned. This arrangement is entirely unacceptable. If you've billeting to do, I suggest you billet in rebel households. Aye, there's a fine idea. I shall speak to the governor this very morning on the matter."

"You'll have to ferry yourself to Castle Island," Dudley said, "or take your complaint to Col. Leslie. He's been appointed acting governor of the colony."

"When did this happen?"

"Very recently. By the by, I may decide to issue Writs of Assistance on all your ships and confiscate everything you own. And while you rot in prison, who would tend your pretty wife and daughter?"

Winslow purpled with anger. Mrs. Winslow went ashen.

"It is settled, then," Dudley said. "We'll expect supper at six o'clock. I prefer beef to mutton, unless . . ."

He sniffed the air.

"What's that I smell? You, girl, tell me. What is it you've got in the kitchen?"

"Roast duck, my lord," Rachel said.

"Jolly good. We'll have roast duck at six. What's your name?"

"Rachel, my lord."

"By Jove, you're a pretty one. I should like very much to see more of you. Fetch us some water upstairs."

Rachel glanced at her father, who grudgingly nodded his assent. With a curtsy she retreated to the kitchen and hurried outdoors to the well. Minutes later she was mounting the staircase with a porcelain pitcher of water balanced on a tray. In her father's bedchamber she found Dudley peering through the window's lace curtain.

"Perfect," he was saying to Bradshaw. "There's the Green Dragon tavern just down the street. You can see everyone coming and going."

"My lord is certain the rebel meeting is tonight?" Bradshaw said.

"I have it on the best authority. We'll bag the scoundrels this very evening and see them hanging from a gallows on the morrow."

Rachel gasped. Her brother Robert had mentioned the Green Dragon only two nights before. Water spilled from the pitcher and splashed across the floor.

"Blast you, clumsy girl," Dudley said. "Put it down over there and be gone with you."

"Aye, my lord."

She left the tray on a side table and retreated.

"Wait," Dudley said. She halted in the doorway.

"Bradshaw, what say you?" Dudley said. "Is she not the prettiest wench you've seen in this miserable town?"

"Indeed, my lord."

"What's your name, girl?"

"It has not changed since last we spoke, my lord."

"Don't get tart with me," Dudley said. "Tell me your name."

"Winslow."

"No, no, I know well enough your surname. Tell me your Christian name."

"Rachel."

"You'll serve us dinner, won't you, pretty Rachel?"

"If my lord wishes it."

Sgt. Hodges nudged her aside and squeezed through the door.

"Where will you be wanting your trunks, my lord?" he said.

"Set them by the bed, and put my writing things on the desk. Oh—and have the men mustered at eight o'clock sharp. We've a little jaunt this evening."

"Aye, my lord. There's just one difficulty."

"What the devil do you mean?"

"The men," Hodges said. "I'm not sure they'll keep their wits about them after dark."

"Why not?"

"Malone's got the whole regiment spooked with his ghost."

"Ghost?"

"The one he chased last night, my lord."

"You don't mean that silly business in the King's Chapel graveyard?"

"Indeed I do, my lord. Malone says he saw the spirit of Regina Silsby slip right through the sod. Says she left her cloak behind, and that she'll come up again a'looking for it—maybe tonight. She's a ghost, she is. That's what he says. O'Toole was with him. He saw her, too—swears she pulled the boot right off his foot trying to drag him down into the grave with her. And she's left an image of her face at the gravesite. It's got them all scared as schoolboys."

"They'll do their duty," Dudley said, "or feel a lash on their backs."

"There's things even a lash won't tame, my lord. The lads are scared, they are, and that's gospel truth."

"Preposterous."

Rachel slipped into the hall, amazed. How could an entire regiment be frightened of her? Down the stairs she padded and through the kitchen door to the stable yard.

"Think, think," she said, stroking the scab on her brow. What had her brother whispered to her about the Green Dragon? Aye, that was it—he would sup there with Boston's most influential men. Sons of Liberty? Surely not. Robert had always been a timid sort, not one to romp about with his face painted and his hair sprouting feathers. But since he had been apprenticed to Josiah Sinquin the jeweler, he was concocting all manner of fables about Indian war parties and midnight raids on king's agents. He must have joined himself to the rebels. And this very night the king's agents would raid their meeting at the Green Dragon and follow it with a hanging on the morrow.

"He is so young," she said aloud. The thought of seeing him in his grave made her cringe. She must warn him, but how? It was baking day, and she would be confined to the kitchen until nightfall. Besides, there was the roast duck and the plum pudding to mind, and four officers expecting dinner at six o'clock. Her mother would never allow her to run an errand outside the house. She would not be free until bedtime, long after the soldiers had finished their sordid raid.

Perhaps she should tell her father. But what could he do? If he intervened, Capt. Dudley might easily issue Writs of Assistance and confiscate all his property. Her father would be thrown into prison, and she and her mother cast into the street, along with her grandfather. How could she choose between her brother's death and her family's ruin?

Her eyes wandered to her feet, where the muddy snow was holed by hoof marks.

"What on earth . . ." she wondered. White grass was sprouting from a trampled heap. She tugged the woolen sprigs and lifted her father's wig from the mud. It was mangled worse than a banshee's tresses. Not even a corpse would possess a mane so disheveled. She was about to toss the hairpiece aside when an impish idea struck her.

"Frightened as schoolboys," she said, studying the wig. "I wonder . . ."

It might just work. But her scheme would require more than a soiled wig to succeed.

"Robert's apron," she said. The leather garment also lay somewhere in the yard. Her brother had used it to polish pewter and silver, but the thing had grown too worn to serve him well. He had tossed it into the mud for the goat to gobble. Perhaps it still lay where he had cast it. She rushed to the sheep pen and dragged a rake through the mire.

"Hah," she said when at last she lifted the rag from a bog of black filth. Its leather was more withered than the ugliest witch's hide. Bruises of black and blue scarred the skin as if a thousand mallets had bludgeoned its owner to death. Fetid odors seeped from it.

She rinsed it with the wig in a pail of well water and headed back to the house.

"These will do nicely," she said.

Three

Regina Silsby Returns

In the shadow of the Green Dragon tavern Rachel stood rubbing her shoulders for warmth. The inn was a large house of red brick with dormer windows lining its sloped roof. A muddy yard spotted with snow separated the house from the stable and kitchen.

On most evenings Rachel would have been in her room reading her Scriptures before retiring. But this night she had fashioned her bedding into a ladder, as Peter Slater had done, and descended to the woodpile beneath her window. The logs formed a rough staircase to the ground, and from there she had slipped through the back gate of the garden.

Distant church bells struck three-quarters past eight o'clock. She leaned against the tavern wall, praying a hundredth time for protection and wondering if God would answer. Even the elements seemed to doubt it. The moon hid its face behind a veil of cloud, and all of heaven's stars fled away with it. Trees hurled snow and ice about with mocking glee.

From the folds of her cloak she fished her brother's apron. Despite several washings, the leather smelled more foul than barnyard muck. She had cut two eye holes into the wrinkled skin and fashioned a mouth of shredded strips like broken teeth. With a mixture of soot and lard she had blackened both eye sockets. The effect was ghastly.

Carefully she fitted the mask over her head. It gripped her face like a clammy octopus, and the stench sickened her. She tightened the laces she had stitched down the back of the scalp, and let the cords dangle behind her neck. From a cape pocket she retrieved her father's wig. After donning the hairpiece, she completed her disguise by shrouding her head in the hood of her cloak.

A dark window enabled her to inspect her reflection. Leering from the glass was a grisly skull flecked with rotting skin. Its mouth was a ragged tangle of decay. She shuddered, even though she knew she was gazing at herself.

Beside the inn stood an open wagon. She climbed to the driver's box and peered through a lighted window. On the room's far wall blazed a great stone hearth. Two tables were heaped with steaming platters of beef, duck, quail, venison, mutton, and fish. There were trays of potatoes, squash, pumpkin, beans, and bread, and pots of pease pudding as well. A dozen tradesmen surrounded the tables, washing down gluttonous mouthfuls with strong ale. Stabbing fingers and pounding fists punctuated their discussion.

By the fire sat her father's friend, John Hancock. Why the elegantly tailored gentleman would associate with craftsmen and common tradesmen escaped her. Josiah Sinquin seemed equally out of place in a peach-colored coat of rich brocade. Her brother Robert was perched on a stool at Sinquin's side, his eyes drooping with fatigue.

Rachel stood on tiptoes and pressed an ear to the window.

"Hear me well, Mr. Hancock," said a short, rotund fellow. "A tyrant will always disarm the populace first, and then work his will on them."

"Really, Adams," Hancock said. "Will the British army confiscate every fowling piece in the colony?"

"Muskets are useless without gunpowder," Adams said. "Mark my words: they will steal our powder. Without weapons we are defenseless. Armed, we are invincible."

"Where is the militia's powder just now?" Hancock said. All eyes turned to a stocky man seated opposite Robert.

"Revere?" Adams said to him.

"Portsmouth," Revere said, "at Fort William and Mary. And we have another store hidden nearby."

"Whereabouts?" Hancock said. Revere glanced at Adams, who nodded his assent.

"Pembroke farm," Revere said.

"Pembroke?" Hancock said. "So, the old sot has agreed to help us after all, has he? Jolly good of him. How much?"

"Six kegs," Revere said. "The rest are in Portsmouth."

"Who knows of it?"

"Of Pembroke, none, save us. Everyone knows about Portsmouth."

"We'll have to remove it from the fort," Adams said. "We can send everything to Pembroke and distribute it among the local militias from there."

"When?" Revere said.

Rachel felt something prod her leg. She whirled about, expecting the night watchman. A dog was sniffing her skirt.

"Good gracious," she said. "Where did you come from?"

The hound gazed balefully at her.

"Go away," she said. "Shoo. Back to the barn, where you belong."

The dog sat on his haunches, cocked back his head, and howled.

"Hush," she said. "For heaven's sake, what ails you? Be gone at once."

She swung a foot at the hound's nose. He retreated several paces, sat down, and howled again. When she glanced back at the window, the tavern men were staring toward her. Sinquin prodded Robert awake and urged him to the glass.

Into the wagon bed she plunged as Robert's face appeared in the pane. He glanced about, then vanished again. Footsteps were soon squashing through the stable yard.

"Stop that infernal noise," he said. "What's got your dander up? There's nothing here."

The animal circled the wagon, sniffing and whining. Robert grabbed the dog by the scruff of his neck and dragged him to the stable.

"Fetch me out here in the freezing cold, will you?" he said. "I'll show you."

He shoved the dog into the stable and latched shut the door. The hound continued baying from the barn.

Minutes passed before the animal quieted. Rachel lifted her eyes above the wagon rail and scanned the deserted stable yard. Suddenly her body began quaking with cold. Even the wagon rattled. She descended to the ground and paced the tavern wall, rubbing her arms and stamping her feet, hoping to stir the blood in her limbs. Even her mask was growing stiff. She touched her fingers to her face and felt ice crystals forming on the leather.

Church bells struck nine o'clock. Half gone was the night, and not a single British soldier had appeared. Her shoulders drooped. She must have mistaken Dudley's intentions. If the Green Dragon had been his target, his soldiers would have already arrived. There was no threat of a raid, no danger of a hanging. For naught she had fashioned a ridiculous, foul-smelling mask and stood freezing in a dank Boston barnyard.

"Have I made a fool of myself?" she said. "What am I but a witless girl who ought to be home abed."

She loosened the laces at her neck and tugged off the mask and wig. Her cheeks were chafed, and her brow throbbed. The leather's stench lingered on her skin and hair, sickening her.

"Idiot," she said, and hurled her disguise to the ground.

Boots shuffled in the street. Her heartbeat quickened. She scooted to the fence and peered down the lane. Four soldiers were slinking toward the tavern. An officer, unmistakable with his long sword, tramped alongside them. Brass glinted in his belt. He was carrying a pistol.

"Mercy," she said, and rushed to retrieve her mask. As she wriggled back into it, a fifth soldier emerged from beneath the tavern steps.

"Well?" said the officer. The voice was Capt. Dudley's.

"I have been watching them from that window, my lord," Sgt. Hodges said. He indicated a pane just around the corner from Rachel's perch.

"How many?" Dudley said.

"All of them, my lord."

"Here's a bit of luck. We'll net the whole gaggle with a single cast. You men post yourselves at the door. Malone, take the others and secure the back gate."

The soldiers tramped past Rachel's hiding place.

"When she struck that branch with her wand," said Malone, "it dropped off like a ripe apple. Almost killed me and O'Toole with it, she did. Then she disappeared into her grave. Walked straight into it, like she was descending into a pond. But it was solid ground. Not even the snow was disturbed. And that face . . ."

"Hush, men," Dudley said.

"The ghost, my lord," someone said. "Malone was a'telling us—"

"Quiet."

"She's close about," Malone said. "There's death in the air. You can smell it."

" 'Tis a bad omen," said another. "Men and beasts we can fight, but demons?"

The others grumbled their assent.

"Enough of this nonsense," Dudley said. "Fix bayonets."

"What good's a bayonet or musket against witchery?" Malone said.

"Do as I say, at once."

Steel clattered as the soldiers clamped their pikes to their weapons. A swath of light suddenly brightened the tavern doorway. Josiah Sinquin and Robert stepped through the entry.

"Here's a pretty pair of rascals," Dudley said, brandishing his sword. "You, there. Halt, in the name of the king."

The pair stiffened.

"Cursed Sons of Liberty," Dudley said. " 'Twill be the gallows for you. Arrest them."

Rachel clutched a hand to her throat. She had planned to show herself and frighten away the soldiers. Now the scheme seemed like childish folly.

"Who's there?" Dudley said, staring her way. "You, by the fence, show yourself."

She could not move. Fear had frozen her feet to the ground. Dudley marched toward her, sword flashing. At last her legs awakened and she stumbled backward. Across the yard she tripped and staggered, finally thudding against the barn. Her fingers floundered with the latch at her back and the door swung open. She tumbled inside and slammed the door.

The stable was pitch black. Along the rough planks she groped, and fell panting into an empty stall. The barn door kicked open.

"Let none of those villains escape," Dudley said. "I'll bring this one."

He strutted into the stable.

"Come out," he said, "or I shall run you through."

Rachel struggled to silence her frantic breathing. She squeezed into a corner, hoping she might melt through the beams. Perhaps the captain would mistake her for a heap of straw. As she debated diving into a mound, Dudley's grim figure blocked the stall.

"Show yourself," he said, "or I will kill you."

A strange frenzy seized her. The paralyzing dread suddenly exploded into rage. Her face contorted into a snarl, and her fingers spread into claws. Fury fired her limbs. She lunged at him, almost clubbing his nose with her brow. A lion's roar blasted from her throat.

Dudley yelped and fell backward. She leapt over him and bounded for the doorway. A hapless soldier crossed her path. It was Malone. She thrust her withered face in front of his.

"The ghost," he bellowed. "Regina Silsby!"

"Shoot her," Dudley howled. Malone dropped his gun and bolted. The remaining soldiers leveled quaking muskets at her. Three thunderclaps boomed. Flashes brightened the barn and smoke billowed through the doorway. When the haze cleared the ghost was gone.

❧

"Did you see that?" one soldier said. "She was a bloody corpse."

"My shot went right through her," said another. "I couldn't have missed."

"Fools," Dudley said, stumbling through the barn entry. "Don't let any of those rascals escape."

Already Josiah Sinquin and Robert were dashing into an alley. Adams, Hancock, and the others spilled from the inn and scattered.

"Arrest them," Dudley said. "Malone, get your carcass over here. Hodges, where are you?"

Windows facing the street opened. Nightcapped men and women peered into the barnyard.

"Confound you dogs," Dudley said. "Round them up. Don't lose them."

The soldiers scrambled to obey, leaving Dudley alone.

"You there, lobster-back," called a man from across the street. "What's got into you?"

"Someone's been shot," a neighbor said.

Down the lane dashed the night watchman, his lantern bobbing on a long pike.

"I heard shots," he said.

"Them lobster-backs have killed a man."

Doors along the street banged open. Half-dressed men converged on the tavern with torches and pitchforks.

"That lobster-back shot someone," onlookers said.

"Fetch a doctor. There's a man hurt."

"Set this redcoat up on a rail. It's tar and feathers for him."

"I say we hang him."

Dudley tugged free his pistol and swept it over the gathering crowd.

"I'll shoot the first man who draws near," he said.

"Which one of us will you be murdering, redcoat?" someone said. "You've one shot against a hundred souls."

In the barn doorway appeared a man waving Dudley's sword.

"See what I've got," he said. "I'll have that lobster-back's heart on his own skewer."

"Stand back," the night watchman said. "This man is in my custody. No one harms him."

"Tory! Lobster lover!"

"Stand back, I say. Captain, you are hereby cited for disturbing the peace and inciting a riot."

"You are citing me?" Dudley said.

" 'Twas you and your soldiers that started this disturbance," the watchman said. "You'll come with me, please, to the magistrate's offices."

"Finish him here," shouted the mob. "Have done with him now. He's killed a man."

"Who's been shot?" the watchman said. "Show me. Do you see a man down? Tell me where he is."

The crowd grew sullen.

"To your homes then, all of you," the watchman said. "To your homes, I say. Captain, you'll come with me, please."

"How dare you order me about. I am here on the king's business."

"Show some sense, man. Would you rather be torn limb from limb? Put up your pistol. And for your own safety's sake, Captain, I must insist that you accompany me."

"Do you know who I am?"

"You're a man ready to lose his life. Do as I say, sir, or prepare to breathe your last."

Fuming, Dudley uncocked his pistol and shoved it back into his belt.

"Away with him," the crowd shouted. "Put him in the stocks."

"Stand aside," the watchman said. "Stand aside, all of you."

With his pike he cleared a passage through the crowd.

"To your homes," he said. "Make way."

The mob parted, and the watchman led Dudley through the jeering crowd.

From a corner of the barn Rachel watched the commotion. She had tripped backward into the barn as the guns had discharged, and their shots had passed harmlessly over her head. Amazed and unhurt, she had scrambled into a dark corner. Now, with the crowd swelling and Dudley departing, her danger was past.

She wiped a relieved hand across her brow. Coarse leather scratched her fingers. She was still garbed as a ghost. Quickly she yanked the mask and wig from her head and hid them in the folds of her cloak. Fresh air filled her lungs. How sweet it smelled! She smoothed her hair and skirts and joined the crowd following Dudley down the street.

Four

❦

Gossip

"Regina Silsby's ghost, indeed," Rachel's mother said. She sat by the drawing room's bay window with Abigail Sutton's mother and Widow Hawkins. Spread over a table before the women was an enormous, half-finished quilt. Rachel practiced her music lessons at the clavichord while Abigail shared the bench with her, working her cross-stitching.

"How else do you explain it?" Mrs. Sutton said. "Josiah Sinquin himself saw her. So did your son, Robert."

"I remember the Drury hauntings," Widow Hawkins said. "That farm was plagued with witchery."

"A daughter, wasn't it?" Mrs. Sutton said.

"Aye," the old woman said. "Murdered in the upper room, she was. The mistress herself told me she saw the spirit many a time, still covered with blood and—"

"For heaven's sake, madame," Mrs. Winslow said.

"Come, Sarah, even you must admit that in life Regina Silsby was a very strange woman."

"She was merely eccentric," Mrs. Winslow said. "That is hardly—"

"Mother," Rachel said, "did you know Regina Silsby?"

"Mercy, child. That is her portrait hanging over the clavichord there."

Rachel gasped. Gazing from the framed canvas above the instrument was a beautiful young woman with coils of dark hair cascading to her waist. In one hand she cradled a quill pen and in the other a sheet of music. Curling her lips was a hint of a smile—a mischievous smile, Rachel thought.

"That clavichord belonged to her as well," Mrs. Winslow said.

"No," Rachel said, withdrawing her fingers from the keys. "Why is it here?"

"She was my aunt, dear. Your grandfather's sister, for a fact."

"But, Mother, I always thought this portrait was of you."

"We did look very much alike. I daresay you resemble her even more than I."

"Why did you never mention her before?"

"Until this week, there was no need. I hardly knew her really. She died when I was but a child."

"I remember her," Widow Hawkins said. "She played the King's Chapel organ as sweetly as yourself, Rachel."

"Aye," Mrs. Winslow agreed. "Aunt Regina was a gifted woman."

" 'Twas a shame she died so young," Widow Hawkins said. "Unfinished business, that's what brings them back, you know."

"Well," Mrs. Winslow said, "there's no unfinished business to keep Regina Silsby bound to earth."

"Except, perhaps . . ."

A stern gaze from Mrs. Winslow stopped her.

"No, I suppose not," the old woman said, returning to her needlework.

"Do tell us, madame," Abigail urged her.

"Nonsense," Mrs. Winslow said. "Abigail, we'll have a lesson from the Scriptures, if you please. Be kind enough to read to us, dear."

"Certainly, madame," Abigail said, disappointed.

"I remember the happenings at Carrington Hall," Widow Hawkins said. "Anna Carrington saw the ghost every autumn solstice, candle in hand, looking for her dead husband. Shot in a duel, he was, and his wife hanged herself in the stairway that very night, much as Regina Silsby did."

"My aunt did not hang herself," Mrs. Winslow said.

"Flung herself from the King's Chapel choir loft," Widow Hawkins said. "What's the difference? She was just as dead, either way."

"I'll thank you not to spread such rumors."

"Talk to Mr. Newcomb," Widow Hawkins said. "He was a bell ringer at the time. He saw her."

"No more talk of ghosts," Mrs. Winslow said. "Abigail, we'll hear your Scriptures now, if you please."

"Aye, madame."

Abigail cleared her throat and began to read from the Old Testament. *"And Saul disguised himself, and put on other raiment, and he went, and two men with him, and they came to the woman by night: and he said, I pray thee, divine unto me by the familiar spirit, and bring me him up, whom I shall name unto thee. . . . Then said the woman, Whom shall I bring up unto thee? And he said, Bring me up Samuel. And when the woman saw Samuel, she cried with a loud voice: and the woman spake to Saul, saying, Why hast thou deceived me? for thou art Saul."*

"Really, Abigail," Mrs. Winslow said. "Have you no wit? Choose another passage."

"Aye, madame," Abigail said, fanning the pages.

"Someone should seek her out," Mrs. Sutton said.

"Who?" Mrs. Winslow said.

"Regina Silsby, of course, to learn why she has come back. I'm told that Madame Slocum has a familiar spirit. Perhaps she could ask Regina Silsby what it is she wants."

" 'Twas well known what Regina Silsby wanted," Widow Hawkins said.

"Saints alive," Mrs. Winslow said. "You two are positively unchristian. Familiar spirits and ghosts—really. Can you not leave the dead in peace?"

"You cannot hide the truth from your daughter forever," Widow Hawkins said, "especially now that Regina Silsby's ghost has returned."

"Rachel," said a gruff voice from upstairs.

"Oh, bother," Rachel said. "That Capt. Dudley is insufferable."

"Rum, girl," the captain said. "Bring it here at once."

"You beware that fellow, Rachel," Widow Hawkins said. "He's got the evil eye on you. 'Tis the curse of being pretty. Every scoundrel in the colony will be after you."

Rachel grabbed her grandfather's jug and mounted the stairs.

"You expect me to believe," said an unfamiliar voice in her father's room, "that a ghost scared off the king's soldiers?"

"The men are certain that Regina Silsby is haunting the streets of Boston," Dudley said. "I saw her myself, your lordship."

"Dash it all, where is that girl? Ah, there you are, my dear."

Rachel stood in the doorway facing a red-coated officer. His face was weathered and jowled, his frame paunched, his uniform festooned with medallions of gold and silver. A sword dangled at his side. By the window stood Dudley in his shirt sleeves and waistcoat.

"Here's a good girl," the officer said, holding out a mug to her. "Thank you, child."

"May I inquire your name, sir," Rachel said as she poured, "and how you come to be in my father's house unannounced?"

"My, you are a bold one," the officer said. "But you're quite right. Do forgive my bad manners. I am Colonel Leslie, of his majesty's 64th Regiment of Foot. And just recently saddled by the governor with all of his duties as well, confound him. May I ask whom I have the pleasure of addressing?"

"I am Rachel Winslow, my lord."

"Well, you've nothing to fear from me, pretty Rachel," he said. "Now be off about your chores."

"As you wish, my lord."

She retreated to the hallway.

"We cannot have the king's officers blaming their incompetence on ghosts," Leslie told the captain.

"If it please your lordship . . ."

"It does not please my lordship. Roast your liver, Dudley. How could you botch a simple arrest? If your father got wind of this, he'd . . . well, never mind. Some brazen rogue is masquerading as a demon. Find out who it is and arrest him. Once he's unmasked, our men will behave themselves."

"Aye, my lord. I have my sources."

"Make good use of them. You're not an earl yet. Now get yourself dressed and come with me."

"Where are we bound, my lord?"

"I am giving you an opportunity to redeem yourself."

Leslie emerged from the room so suddenly that Rachel jumped. He guzzled the remainder of his rum and plopped the mug into her palm.

"My, you're a pretty one," he said, pinching her cheek.

"Thank you, my lord."

"Rachel, dear," said her mother from the dining room. "Listen. There's the King's Chapel bell. Do you hear?"

The great bronze bell was slowly tolling.

"Somebody's died," her mother said. "Rachel, do you hear?"

"My lord will excuse me," Rachel said. She curtsied and descended the stairs.

"Rachel," Mrs. Winslow said, "run and find out who has died. Abigail, you may accompany her."

"Aye, madame."

The girls hurried to the front hall and grabbed their capes.

"Abigail," Rachel said, "did Widow Hawkins say what it is Regina Silsby wants?"

"Your mother would not let her speak another word about it. Oh, Rachel, I'm dying of curiosity. We simply must find out."

Five

❧

Dangerous Schemes

Rachel and Abigail tramped the cobbled street toward King's Chapel. The air was crisp and cold, the sky threatening rain. If the temperature dropped, it would be snow. All along the lane women swept their front steps while children dumped buckets of refuse into the gutters. At the corner of Water Street Rachel spied Col. Leslie marching with Capt. Dudley toward the harbor. Milling about the docks were British officers chatting and pointing into the bay. For a moment Rachel gazed up Water Street toward King's Chapel.

"A chance to redeem himself," she said, pondering Col. Leslie's words to Dudley. "Abigail, let us see what is acting up at the wharf."

"But your mother is expecting news from the chapel."

"We shall go there afterwards."

"I know that look on your face. You're up to mischief."

"Not at all. Perhaps one of my father's ships is arriving. Come along."

" 'Tis a fool's errand you're on, Rachel Winslow."

"Good morrow, ladies," a fishmonger said. "Here's fresh cod, fresh haddock, just come in from the ferry ways."

"Oys! Fine oys," said a nearby oysterman. Beyond his cart stretched a line of wagons piled with fish, mollusks, bread, and meat. Vendors bawled their wares and prices. Tapping hammers, creaking looms, and grinding machinery echoed through the shops along the wharf. A great iron pot of boiling soap foamed before the open door of the sail maker's loft, where sheets of canvas hung from the rafters. Wagons trundled behind clopping horses and cracking whips. Gangs of slaves wrestled hogshead casks into the counting houses, taverns, and shops. Masters and merchants shouted orders, argued terms, tallied accounts, and traded coins. The air reeked of fish, tar, hemp, brine, and resin. Gulls shrieked overhead, and from the distant headlands boomed a thunder of ocean surf.

"Look there," Abigail said, tugging Rachel's sleeve. "Yonder comes Josiah Sinquin, the jeweler. Is he not handsome?"

"And he's seen the ghost," Rachel said, "or so your mother tells us."

Josiah Sinquin, wearing a topcoat of fine purple over his silk waistcoat and breeches, was bowing a greeting to Joshua Wyeth, the coppersmith. Sinquin's white wig contrasted sharply with Wyeth's dull brown locks, and the jeweler's elegant tricornered hat sprouted a splendid, feathered cockade. Together the two men ambled through the market.

"Speak the truth now, Josiah," Wyeth was saying as the pair approached the girls. "Are you quite certain it was she?"

"With my own eyes I saw her," Sinquin said. "Absolutely ghastly."

He pressed a lace handkerchief to his nostrils.

"Regina Silsby's ghost," Wyeth said. "Simply astounding. Were anyone else telling such a tale I would not believe him. But you, sir . . ."

"Brave Capt. Dudley saw her as well, though he'll be loathe to admit it."

"All Boston is buzzing about his folly. I'm told his troops fired upon her."

"Three rounds," Sinquin said. "The musket balls passed straight through her without effect. That very same moment she vanished."

"Completely?"

"I saw it myself. A flash and a bang and the ghost was gone."

"You think that she is really a spirit?"

"Upon my word," Sinquin said, "I am almost inclined to believe she is."

"But surely, sir, she must be . . . well, *somebody*."

"One look at her face is enough to make a breathing man doubt it. If she's not a ghost, she's the ugliest hag this side of Hades."

"Excuse me, good sirs," Rachel said, "but you speak of Regina Silsby, do you not?"

"Why, bless my soul," Sinquin said. " 'Tis my young apprentice's fair sister. A fine day to you, Miss Rachel, and to your sweet friend there."

"Were you gentlemen talking of Regina Silsby just now?" Rachel said. "Was she really so hideous as you say?"

"Ah, Rachel," he said, " 'tis not a tale for a young girl's ear."

"I am almost seventeen. Surely that is grown enough to bear a shock or two."

"You must run along home, lass. Your mother will worry about you."

"We shan't escape the ghost at home. Regina Silsby is on every tongue in my mother's parlor. But you, Mr. Sinquin, you have seen her. What did she look like?"

"Rachel, I am glad we happened upon each other."

He took her arm and steered her toward the wharf.

"Your brother is a fine apprentice," he said. "He speaks of you quite often. Rachel, Rachel, Rachel. . . . 'Tis all I ever hear."

"I am flattered."

"He must have told you that my business fares well."

"Indeed, Mr. Sinquin, and your attire testifies quite boldly of your prosperity. Even Mr. Hancock does not dress so finely as you."

" 'Tis a good life I'm blessed to enjoy. There's just one thing missing."

"What is that?"

"Rachel," he said, taking her hand, "I believe I am ready to marry."

"How . . . wonderful for you."

"I should like very much if you would permit me to call upon your father to discuss the matter."

"My father? Mercy, Mr. Sinquin, you don't mean . . . that is to say . . . well, really . . ."

"Come, Rachel, you said you could take a shock or two. Would I make so horrible a husband as that? 'Twill be a comfortable life you'll live with me. Business is good and bound to get better, what with all that's acting up these days. I can cover you with all sorts of pretty little trinkets. Why, see here."

He drew a leather pouch from a pocket and dumped its contents into his palm.

"Look, Rachel," he said, stirring two glittering green stones with a finger, "emeralds from the Indies. Only last week I got them. A pretty pair of earrings they'll make."

"Oh, Mr. Sinquin, they are beautiful."

"They shall be yours then. I'll fashion the finest earrings this side of the Atlantic."

"Mr. Sinquin, really, I could not ask you to . . ."

"Tut, tut. I'll bring them with me when I call on your father. Soon I'll have you dripping in jewelry, Rachel. You'll be the finest advertisement to my business. A pretty wife who roams Boston sparkling like the stars. We'll have a grand house, lots of servants, a coach-and-four and . . . Oh, do say you'll marry me, Rachel."

"Mr. Sinquin, this is so . . . sudden."

"You don't like them," he said, pocketing the gemstones.

"No, no, not at all. They are wonderful, of course. It is just that . . ."

"Excellent," he said. "You've made me the happiest man in all Boston. I'll call on your father the moment they're done. Oh, Rachel, we will be so happy together. You'll see."

He swept off his hat and bowed low, then turned on his heel and pranced down the street.

"God bless you, pretty Rachel," he said over his shoulder.

"Good heavens," Abigail said as she shuffled to Rachel's side. "What on earth has passed between you two just now? Are you keeping secrets from me?"

Rachel watched Sinquin disappear. Handsome indeed he was and master of a thriving business. Visions of plush parlors and sumptuous feasts teased her, of sparkling necklaces and heavy bracelets, of silk gowns studded with pearls and gemstones. Elegant, fawning guests surrounded her, all of them sipping sweet punches and tasting delicate finger cakes, while hired quartets played music in endless gardens. It would have been an alluring picture, if only Sinquin were not so . . .

"Hah," said a familiar voice from beneath the wharf. "If you can do better than that, I'll eat my hat."

Rachel peered under the dock. Low tide had exposed a bed of rocks dripping with slime and barnacles. At the water's edge stood her brother and Peter Slater. They were throwing a dirk into the wharf's soggy pilings.

"Robert," she said. "Hello there, Robert."

He gaped at her.

"For pity's sake, Rachel," he said, "don't cry out so loudly."

She descended the stone steps beside the jetty.

"Rachel, you mustn't go down there," Abigail said. "It is filthy."

"I shall be all right. Robert, whatever are you doing?"

"Peter Slater thinks he can throw better than I."

"And so I shall," Peter said, prying the dirk from the wood. "Watch me, Rachel. I'll pitch this dirk straight into the center of that piling."

"Oh, Rachel," Robert said, squeezing her shoulders, "how I wish you could have seen those lobster-backs run last night. They were almost as fast as Mr. Sinquin and myself."

"Did you frighten them?"

"Certainly not. 'Twas Regina Silsby that set them to flight. I saw her, Rachel, I saw her."

"Really? Was she pretty?"

"Uglier than a sick man's dreams. The redcoats fired three shots straight through her. She was gone before they struck."

"How could she—"

"She's a ghost, Rachel. Don't be so dense."

"Robert, you must get back to your shop. Mr. Sinquin will catch you loafing."

" 'Twas Mr. Sinquin that sent me here. He wants to know what the lobster-backs are saying. Something's acting up."

She peered between the planks above her head. Col. Leslie was strutting back and forth along the dock, his officers pacing after him. The colonel pointed south toward the city gate at Boston Neck.

"Pembroke," he said. "Six kegs of powder. You'll find the rest at Fort William and Mary."

She gasped. The colonel knew of the gun powder.

"Don't stand there staring," Robert said. "We can't do our business with you wandering about. You'll catch every eye on the wharf."

"Would you teach me to throw the dirk?" she said. The boys gawked at her, then laughed.

"Why, in heaven's name?" Peter said. "Will you pin your chickens to the kitchen wall before you gut them? Go home, girl, to your cooking pots and your needlework."

"Very well," she said, "since you're afraid I'll show you up . . ."

"Afraid? Saints alive, Robert, I do believe we've been challenged, and by a lass at that. Go on, let her try."

"Aye, we'll have a merry jest," Robert said. "Here, Rachel, hold the dirk by the tip, like so. No, no, not that way. Look here."

She was only half-listening. Her ear was trained on the British officers treading the wharf above.

"Six men should be enough, my lord," one officer told the colonel. "We'll have every keg stowed at the South Battery before sunrise."

"Very good, Lieutenant. Capt. Dudley here will lead the detachment. You're to arrest that Pembroke rebel as well. Understand? We'll make a lesson of him."

"Rachel, you're not paying attention," Robert said. "Hold the tip of the blade thus."

She blinked her confusion, then took the dirk he offered her.

"No, Rachel, not that way. Goodness, you're as deaf as this dock. Hold it thus."

He pinched her fingers around the blade's tip.

"Now flick the blade with your fingers when you throw it," Robert said. "A good cast will travel straight to the target."

She faced the pillar. After a deep breath she flung the blade toward the piling. The dirk spun wildly, banged against the wood, and clattered among the rocks. The boys howled.

"She'll never make a go of it," Peter said.

"There's a fine spectacle," said a voice from the pier. Two British officers were gazing down at them. Rachel blushed and wiped her hands.

"I could have managed it," she said, "with more practice."

"Rachel, child," Col. Leslie said. "What are you doing down there? Do you know these ruffians?"

"This one is my brother, sir."

"How does a blossom like you come by this briar of a brother? Come up away from there, girl, and get you home. You'll come to no good around the likes of those urchins."

She climbed the stone steps to the pavement.

" 'Twill be a cold day in July," said one officer, "when I see a girl throw a dagger."

The others laughed.

"Back to your kitchen, child," Col. Leslie said. "By the smell of your cooking, I expect you'll have a happy husband sharing your table before long."

"As you say, my lord."

"Off you go, lass, and take your friend with you. There's a good girl. Capt. Dudley, you'll come with me, please. We've other matters to discuss."

The soldiers disappeared into the market.

"Hold, Rachel," Peter said, mounting the stone steps. "You lost your wager to us, and now you must pay your debt."

"I made no wager," she said.

"You couldn't throw the dirk, and so lost the contest."

"I asked you to teach me. It is hardly the same thing."

"You called our courage to question. 'Tis a matter of honor, and now you must make restitution. I'll have a kiss as payment."

"You'll have no such thing," she said. "Come, Abigail, let us be gone. Robert, I trust you have a good report for Mr. Sinquin?"

"For once that peacock is wrong," he said. "The redcoats are up to nothing, and I shall tell him so."

"Would not Mr. Sinquin wish to know that Col. Leslie is sending six soldiers to Pembroke farm?"

"Whatever for?"

"To steal the—"

She bit off the sentence.

"Well?" he said.

"I'm sure I couldn't say. But you had better tell him."

"Why should I get my ears boxed? I heard nothing of the sort, and I stood by you the entire time. Peter, lad, did you hear any talk of the lobster-backs journeying to Pembroke farm?"

"Not a word, but she couldn't hear your lessons on throwing the dirk aright."

"I tell you," she said, "that Col. Leslie is sending six soldiers to arrest Mr. Pembroke and to steal something from him. If you know what's good for you, you'll inform Mr. Sinquin straightaway."

"You're mad, Rachel. Go back home to your kitchen."

With an exasperated groan she turned and stormed off.

"What incompetence," she said. "Fie on Robert, for botching such an important errand."

"Whatever are you jabbering about?" Abigail said. Rachel was too angry to answer. Up the street she marched, not stopping until she had stomped into her house's front hall and banged shut the door.

"Rachel, dear, is that you?" her mother said from the drawing room. "What's the news?"

"News, Mother?"

"Who is it that's died?"

"Died?"

"Heavens, child. Why did you run outside, but to learn for whom the King's Chapel has tolled?"

"Oh. I completely forgot."

"Where have you been for the last hour?"

"I'm sorry, Mother, I was . . . distracted. Please excuse me."

She mounted the stairs, leaving Abigail standing open-mouthed in the front hall. Somehow Mr. Sinquin must get word of the soldiers' trip to Pembroke farm. At the door to her father's study she paused. His writing desk was open, its cubbies neatly stocked with paper, ink, and sealing wax. Perhaps a letter would suffice. But no, a written note might fall into the wrong hands.

"Rachel," said her mother, "you'll stoke the kitchen fire, please. We must start on supper."

There would be no time to visit the jeweler's shop. She pondered alternatives while toying with a letter opener from one of the cubbyholes. Its long, slender blade more resembled a dagger than a paper cutter. On the crest of the silver handle was a pair of ornate initials: RS.

Regina Silsby.

Rachel dropped the letter opener and retreated from the desk. On the wall a framed portrait of her mother gazed at her. Or was it her dead aunt? With dark eyes the image held her captive in a knowing stare, as if attempting to share secret thoughts.

"Why," Rachel wondered aloud, "did you throw yourself from the choir loft?"

Once more she studied the letter opener. Its workmanship was exquisite, its balance perfect. Delicate scrolls adorned its handle, and the blade was surprisingly sharp. She slipped it into a pocket and retreated from the room.

Dying embers still glowed in the kitchen hearth. With kindling and cordwood she coaxed them into a blaze. Soon the kettle and teapot were brimming with water, their fat bellies scorched by flames. Her immediate chores done, she threw on a shawl and stepped outside to the stable.

Odors of musk and meal scented the barn's twilight. Two milk cows munched hay, while sheep and pigs languished in their pens. A chicken coop littered with feathers sheltered a dozen birds.

The stable was framed with posts and trusses similar to the waterfront pilings. She slipped the letter opener from her pocket and pinched the blade between her thumb and finger. With a jerk of her arm she flung it at a pillar behind the door. The blade struck the wood and dropped to the ground. She retrieved it and tried again.

Six

Old Pigot's Tale

Robert Winslow sat hunched at his master's workbench. For the twelfth time he arranged the tools before him, wiping each one clean with a cloth and laying it in the exact spot from which he had taken it. Cluttering the sideboard were projects requiring Sinquin's attention: a pendant needing filigree work, three timepieces awaiting engraved initials, a brooch with a loose pearl. On a bench by the door sat old Pigot, Sinquin's landlord, his grizzled face still wrapped in a woolen shawl and muffler, his lips collapsed over toothless gums.

Down the street came a jaunty thumping of boots. The door flung open, jangling the bell that hung from the lintel.

Josiah Sinquin marched into the shop amidst a swirl of snow. His pockets clattered with coins.

"Well," Pigot said. " 'Tis high time you showed your face in this museum you call a shop."

"A very good afternoon to you, Mr. Pigot," Sinquin said while peeling off his hat and coat. "I was just by your offices in search of you."

"If that be so, I am King George's stepsister. Where's the rent money you promised me?"

"Upon my word, sir, I've three days yet before it's due."

"A week overdue is what you are."

"Is today not the eighth?"

"You know very well what day and week it is. Show me some silver, or your next landlord shall be the jailor."

Sinquin fished several coins from a pocket and tossed them on the table.

"English shillings," Pigot said, squinting at the money. "Heaven knows where you get them. Mutton, wool, and chickens is all I'm paid by most folk."

"I am a successful man of business," Sinquin said.

"Business? The only person I ever see toiling hereabouts is that apprentice of yours."

"Stay a while and you'll see some work done. Robert, make yourself useful and boil some water. We'll have a toddy for our guest."

"Save your rum," Pigot said. "Just keep this silver flowing into my purse is all I ask. Upon my mother's grave, 'tis the wrong business I'm in. You're faring better than even Revere and Flagg have managed."

"The good people of Boston respect talent," Sinquin said.

"Your talent lies in fleecing others," Pigot said, rattling the shillings in his hand. "You could steal the locket off Regina Silsby's throat, you could."

"Hang you for mentioning that foul name."

"A heartfelt wish, Mr. Sinquin. But a'fore long you may find yourself dangling in her noose—forever."

"Whatever do you mean?"

Pigot chuckled.

"Word is all over Boston," he said, "that you've seen her ghost."

"I saw her, too," Robert said.

"Silence, boy," Sinquin said. "Aye, so I have seen her, for the first and final time, I pray."

"Pray hard, then, Mr. Sinquin, pray hard. And you too, young Robert. There's evil afoot in Boston, mark my words, evil worse than any seen before."

"Talk sense, man."

Pigot eased back on the bench.

"Too young, the both of you," he said, "to remember Regina Silsby. A witch, she was, of the vilest, blackest sort. Even today there's scores of men still cursed by the spells she cast."

"What sort of spells?" Sinquin said.

"Devilish stuff," Pigot said. "Poverty, illness, scourges, plagues, and death. The King's Chapel still bears the stain of her midnight sorceries."

"I have never heard talk of such evils."

"Sit back, then, Mr. Sinquin, and hear the tragic tale of Regina Silsby. You'll be worse for it."

"I'm sure I can stomach an old wives' tale."

"We'll see if you think so when I'm done."

The old man coughed and spat before continuing.

" 'Twas a time long ago," he said, "when you couldn't find in all New England a woman more beautiful than Regina Silsby. Sunlight itself, she was, and blessed by heaven's own angels. She could play the spinet, the clavichord, and all sorts of stringed instruments as prettily as you please. And when she sat at the King's Chapel organ, you felt yourself surrounded by the majesty of heaven itself. Every Sabbath she played, and many a weekday too, as well as most holidays. So sweet was her music that folks would wander into the chapel from the streets to listen.

"She was to wed the first mate on one of her father's ships. Proctor was his name, Morgan Proctor—a dashing fellow, and destined to do well in the world. But on his last run to the West Indies a gale swept him overboard. Lost at sea he was, poor devil. The news reached Regina Silsby as she practiced at the King's Chapel organ. Stark raving mad she went—tore her hair and ran from the loft shrieking like a lunatic. She shut herself in the attic room of her father's house and wouldn't speak to anyone. Soon after she had a gravestone erected for Morgan Proctor in the King's Chapel cemetery. Every evening she'd visit it, even though he wasn't buried there. Always dressed in black, she was, after that. And the sun in her soul was gone."

"That is understandable," Sinquin said.

"Aye, but Regina Silsby's trespasses had hardly begun. Since God had taken Morgan Proctor from her, she turned to Satan for solace. Many a night, long after decent women were home abed, Regina Silsby would enter the King's Chapel, all alone, to consort with her demons and cast her wicked spells.

Word had it that she was trying to bring Morgan Proctor back from the dead. Into the wee hours she'd play that bewitched organ . . ."

"Come, now, Pigot. How could she play the organ by herself? Someone must pump the bellows."

"You don't say, Mr. Sinquin. That is a mystery, is it not? How did she manage it? Sorcery is what I say: witchcraft and magic of the blackest sort. The very devil danced with her on those dark nights, and evil spirits did her bidding. All Boston heard the sound of their wanton revelry. And those good persons who spoke ill of her soon found themselves sick in their beds, suffering greatly from the vilest maladies."

"If she was bewitching the chapel," Sinquin said, "why did the vicar not expel her?"

"Possessed of an evil spirit, he was. Regina Silsby had him locked in her sorceries. Then one dark November night, while she was making her sordid music, a bloody scream filled the King's Chapel. Townfolk came running, but the chapel doors were bolted shut. Someone finally broke through a window and found Regina Silsby lying dead in the center aisle, eyes wide open and staring at the ceiling. She'd thrown herself from the organ loft and broken her neck on the pavement."

"She killed herself?" Sinquin said.

"Her face was frozen in terror," Pigot said, "like she'd seen the devil himself. Who knows? Maybe she succeeded in bringing Morgan Proctor back, only to find that his risen carcass was too foully eaten by the sea maggots. Well, sir, whatever fiend it was that confronted her that night, it drove her to her death. That bewitched vicar buried her in the King's Chapel cemetery, despite the protests of God-fearing folk. To this day she lies there, polluting that consecrated ground.

Thirty-one years Regina Silsby's been silent. But now she's come back — back from the dead, a'searching for something . . . or someone."

"Someone?" Sinquin said.

Pigot lowered his voice.

"She died unwed," he said, "a'trying to raise up her betrothed. Now's she's buried beside his empty grave, and what I say is: Regina Silsby's looking for a husband to fill it."

"That is absurd, sir. Why search for a husband after so many years?"

"There's many a thing we mortals don't know of the spirit realm," Pigot said. "Were I a man that Regina Silsby's laid eyes upon, I'd take pains not to let her look on me again. What's more, I'd cover myself with every blessing known to God and man. She's powerful, she is, the very devil's daughter."

"I don't believe it," Sinquin said. "I refuse to believe it."

"Suit yourself," Pigot said, rising. "You're the man who's seen her, not I. Only you can say how real she is. But if I was in your place, I would not pass my nights near the King's Chapel graveyard. I daresay I would not venture out-of-doors after sunset. Still, what's to be gained by caution? Regina Silsby could slip into your very bedchamber, if she'd a mind to do it. You may yet wake up some night and find her leering at you from your bedside."

Sinquin swallowed.

"I've got what I came for, at any rate," Pigot said, jingling the coins in his pocket, "and I've spoken my peace, so I'll not speak it again. But heed me well, Josiah Sinquin: some unlucky fellow will be gone to that empty grave with Regina

Silsby before this affair's finished. Consider yourself warned, sir."

He pulled open the door. Icy winds carried snow into the shop.

"A very good day to you, Mr. Sinquin," Pigot said with a grin. He rattled the coins in his pocket and closed the door behind him. Sinquin stood silently by the threshold, watching the snowflakes melt.

"I'll have that toddy, Robert," he said at last. "If old Pigot's not thirsty, I am. Get the water to boiling."

"Aye, sir. Mr. Sinquin, you don't think there's any truth to what Mr. Pigot has said just now?"

Sinquin blinked uncertainly.

"Poppycock," he said. "Aye, that's what it is, pure poppycock. We've more to worry us than a spinster hobgoblin. What's the news from the lobster-backs?"

"News, sir?"

"I sent you to Dobson's Wharf this morning."

"Aye," Robert said. "I nearly forgot. They said nothing of import."

"Nothing at all?"

"On my grandmother's grave—begging your pardon, sir."

"Imbecile," Sinquin bellowed, clubbing Robert's ear. The boy fell across the workbench, scattering tools on the floor.

"You heard nothing of Pembroke farm?" Sinquin said.

"Pem . . . Pembroke?"

"The lobster-backs plan to steal the militia's gunpowder. Had you a mind in that thick skull of yours, you would know of it."

"Aye, sir," Robert said, nursing his bleeding ear.

"Go at once to Wyeth. Tell him that six soldiers will be traveling to Pembroke farm tonight. He's to be ready with horses at Boston Neck after sundown. That leaves you little time. Tell him you're to help with any preparations. And don't fail me, boy."

"No, sir."

Robert fumbled for his cloak and staggered through the door. Sinquin hurled the fire iron after him.

"Fool," he muttered after the boy was gone. He dropped into a chair and dragged off his wig. Snow spattered the windows. He watched the crystals collect on the glass, then turned his gaze to the hearth fire. Down the flue came a woeful moan as fresh winds blew across the chimney mouth. Orange flames licking the pine logs cringed for a moment, then rose to resume their devouring. Resin perfumed the air.

Pigot's story clouded his thoughts.

"Wives' tales," he said aloud. "Fables and folly."

He opened a cluttered desk drawer and lifted out his money box. It was wonderfully heavy. Inside were sovereigns, shillings, and half-crowns. He fingered the coins, then emptied his pockets into the box. There were more where these came from, many more. A year hence he would build his own house and be done with old Pigot. He might even become the richest man in Boston, if things continued as they were . . . and why shouldn't they?

The wall clock struck half-past four. Dusk would soon swallow the last rays of daylight.

"Just enough time for a nap before supper," he said. He propped his feet on the desk and folded his hands across his lap. But his eyes refused to close.

Seven

❦

At Boston Neck

Freezing rain drizzled from the night sky, making the roads slick and slushy. In the archway of the town gate stood a fur-capped sentry, huddling for warmth in the halo of a torch. With chafed hands he clutched the muzzle of his musket, his chin resting on his knuckles. The buzz in his nostrils betrayed that he was dozing.

Beyond the gate a narrow causeway stretched toward the mainland. Beside its rutted cart path loomed the Boston gallows, with a frayed hangman's rope swaying on its crossbeam. Low tide had drained the bay waters from both sides of the causeway, exposing vast plains of soggy mud flats.

Along the road plodded a tired nag towing a wagon. The sentry snorted awake.

"Who goes there?" he said.

"Elias Jude," came the driver's reply. He coughed up a wad of bile and spit it into the mud.

"State your trade," the soldier said.

"Baker. I am here for the morrow's market."

" 'Tis late," the sentry said.

"My horse threw a shoe."

Hacking spasms rattled the baker's frame. The sentry ignored him, lifting the blanket that covered the wagon bed and poking through the baker's wares. He took a loaf of bread and tucked it under an arm.

"Pass," he said.

"That's two pence," said the baker.

"If you would pass, you must pay the toll."

"There is no toll at this gate."

"Tonight there is a toll: one loaf of bread. Now get you gone, before I make it two."

With a grumble the baker urged his horse through the arch. The sentry returned to the torchlight, tore a chunk from his loaf, and gnawed it. After a long gulp of rum from his canteen, he leaned against the brick wall and nodded off.

From the shelter of a nearby doorway Rachel watched. Her face was already masked in leather, her brow hooded by the mangled wig and cloak. Regina Silsby's last foray had taught her to plan better. Already she had scouted several escape routes, including a path across the mud flats. On her back she bore a canvas sack stuffed with useful sundries, and in one fist she carried a darkened lantern. Black gloves warmed her hands. Stitched to the fabric were patches of white cloth arranged to resemble a skeleton's bones. She was proud of their gruesome effect. If events required her to run, she had replaced the petticoats beneath her skirt with a pair of Grandfather's breeches. Her feet were shod in riding boots that buckled at the knee. In a pocket was Regina Silsby's letter opener.

Her plan was simple: frighten Dudley's horses into the mud flats beyond the gate. The soldiers would waste hours freeing themselves and the animals from the mire. By then they would be too frozen and filthy to continue their journey. There was only one snag in her scheme: slipping past the gate guard to the highway beyond. But with the sentry's belly full of bread and rum, the task might prove simpler than expected.

As the sentry's snores resumed, she eased from her hiding place. Down an alley and past a frozen rain barrel she crept, pausing in the shadow of a stout tree. Fifteen yards of open road separated her from the gate. The sentry stood beneath the larger arch, through which wagons and horses passed. Beside it was a smaller tunnel used by pedestrians. Rachel decided she could slip through the narrow passage without disturbing the guard.

But something was wrong. She stood motionless under the tree, wondering what disturbed her. In her mind she retraced her plans and preparations. She checked her pockets, making certain nothing was missing. A quick inspection of her surroundings confirmed that all was quiet.

"What is it?" she said aloud. Hardly had the words left her lips when the answer struck her like a trumpet blast. She had not committed her plan to God. How could she have been so witless? No plan, however well laid out, could succeed without divine consent and blessing.

"I have not yet committed myself," she said. "There is still time to repent of my deed. Should I go home? Tell me what to do."

Her thoughts drifted to the Pembroke family. God did not need an audacious girl's assistance to protect them.

"Lord, take pity on them," she prayed. "How will those children survive without their father? You must help them. Please help them."

A strange calm descended on her. Was it the peace of God, or the ignorance of a fool? There was only one way to know.

"If I do Your bidding," she said, "please bless me. If not, forgive me."

Leaving the tree's shadow, she paced toward the gate. With every step her trepidation mounted. If someone should unexpectedly appear, or if the sentry should awaken, she knew not who would be more terrified. Her skirts rustled loudly as she walked. She slowed to quiet them, prolonging her torturous trek. The archway glowed a pale orange in the torchlight, with frost forming on the masonry. Fine mist puffed from the sentry's nostrils with each breath. His face was sallow, his nose red and dripping with cold. The stubble on his cheeks seemed too sparse to shave. A coarse blanket draped his shoulders, covering most of his crimson tunic. Mud spattered his white breeches, and between his black boots rested the butt of his musket.

On tiptoes Rachel reached the cover of the smaller arch. Through its cramped tunnel she groped, her fingertips sticking to the icy bricks. A wooden door thumped against her outstretched palm. The guard snorted but did not rouse himself. She pressed her shoulder to the panel, but it was stuck fast. Why had she not foreseen a locked gate? Could she slink through the larger arch, under the very nose of the sentry? Probably not. Her fingers wandered over the planks and found an iron bar stretching across the width of the door.

"Dunce," she said. Naturally the bolt would be on her side of the passage, since she was approaching the gate from within the town. A wooden peg protruded from the iron. She heaved against it, forcing the bar back an inch. The rusty surfaces squealed like a startled pig.

"Who goes there?" the guard said. He tramped about the larger arch, then crossed in front of the smaller tunnel without looking inside. Eventually he returned to his post, swallowed another dram of rum, smacked his lips, and went back to his nap.

Rachel sighed her relief. She adjusted her mask, hoping to ease the chafing of her cheeks. The thing was miserably uncomfortable, and still it smelled of the barnyard. Which odor was worse she could not say, whether hog or horse or goat or goose or lamb or cow . . . or mud. At present all were equally odious. She longed to strip the leather from her face, soothe her irritated skin with a soft hand, and breathe deeply the fresh night air. Strands from the wig were constantly tangling her lashes. As often as she brushed the hairs from her brow, they tumbled back into her eyes. The dew that spattered her clothes was crystallizing into ice, and her feet were growing numb with cold. Worse, her discomforts seemed all for naught, since the gate was barred and the tunnel too dark to see anything. Her lantern was growing heavy too. Her lantern . . .

"Such a simpleton I am," she said, thumping a fist against her forehead. She opened one of the lamp's metal doors and let a sliver of light fall on the iron bar. The slab was brown with rust.

"Gracious God," she said, "there must be a way past this door."

A possibility popped into her head. She dug through her sack for her jug of whale oil and poured several dollops on the iron brackets.

Horses' hooves clattered on the cobblestones.

"Halt," shouted the sentry. "Who goes there?"

Rachel clapped shut the lantern.

"Show yourself," the sentry said. From the tunnel she could see only the haunches of three horses and their riders' legs. She decided the guard would hear nothing from the tunnel while attending to the travelers, so she threw her weight against the bolt, ignoring its squeals, and tugged open the door. Down the tunnel she scrambled, emerging moments later outside the gate.

Bleak bogs surrounded her. Man-shaped iron cages dangled from posts nearby, one still encasing a shriveled corpse. Buzzards had pecked away much of its rotted flesh. Beyond the carcass lay a moor of sparse grasses cluttered with shallow, unmarked graves—condemned criminals buried after their executions. Countless tides had eroded the most distant mounds, leaving human bones exposed in the muck. Sea gulls huddled on skulls and ribs, and putrid mud flats stretched to the black waters of Boston Harbor. Winds laced with freezing rain pelted the expanse.

Josiah Sinquin sat atop his horse alongside Wyeth and Robert.

"Humblest apologies, Mr. Sinquin," said the gate guard, "but you may not leave Boston town tonight."

"We've urgent business on the mainland," Sinquin said.

"Col. Leslie's orders. No one's to leave the city, save the king's soldiers and agents."

Sinquin dismounted.

"My good man," he said, "I must protest. Our errand is most important."

"You can run it on the morrow."

"Has Boston become a stockade? Are her citizens suddenly thieves and robbers?"

"If you've a complaint, you may lodge it with Col. Leslie."

"Col. Leslie is not the master of this town."

"He is master to me," the soldier said. "No one passes this gate tonight, by the colonel's own command."

"Perhaps we can reach some sort of arrangement."

"I'll make no arrangement," the guard said. "Not a soul may leave Boston tonight."

Sinquin drew a club and struck him. The sentry crumpled.

"By my faith," Wyeth said. "What the devil are you doing?"

Sinquin grabbed the sentry's musket and searched his pockets. He found a small pouch of coins and pocketed it.

"Robert," he said. "Give me your knife."

"But why?" Robert said.

"Don't quibble, boy, give it."

"Sir, the poor fellow's down."

"And he'll be on his feet again before long. Give me your knife. 'Twill be one less lobster-back to trouble us."

"Mr. Sinquin, you don't mean to—"

"Blast you, boy, he's seen us. We'll all be dangling from that gallows yonder if we don't finish him."

Robert's jaw flapped, but no sound came out. Sinquin marched to his side and slammed a fist into his belly. The boy tumbled from his saddle, and Sinquin yanked free the knife.

"Really, Josiah," Wyeth said, "you cannot be serious."

" 'Twill look like a simple robbery."

"But to kill the poor fellow."

"Would you rather have a noose about your own neck? You're in this to the gills, Wyeth, whether you want it or not."

He turned on the fallen sentry, knife in hand. Before he could strike, a glowing orb in the graveyard arrested his attention. The object floated from the burial mounds to the road.

"Heavens, what's that?" Wyeth said. He, too, saw the apparition. Sinquin blinked and rubbed his eyes. The light was drifting toward him. Gashes and cavities scarred its surface, and gradually the specter became a human head. But it was severed from its body, floating in midair. And it was glowing. Wild eyes leered at him from withered sockets.

"Sacred thunder," he said. "Regina Silsby."

He fumbled with the musket and jerked the trigger. Nothing happened.

"Cursed firelock," he said. With a flash and a roar the weapon discharged into the cobblestones.

Wyeth's terrified steed bolted away with him. The other horses followed. Robert struggled to his feet, unable to tear his gaze from the monstrous face. The demon fixed her eyes on him. A grin stretched her ragged lips. He shrieked and fled, stumbling as he went. Sinquin threw aside the musket and pounded after him.

Rachel watched the three men vanish, then closed the face plate of her lantern. She had learned the trick as a child from her grandfather. At play in the barn he would often pop open a single panel of his lantern and shine the light upward onto his face. She would scream and scurry from him, only to return begging for more. Now she was using his trick to frighten others, and doubting very much they would seek a second thrill.

Low moans sounded from the archway.

"Mercy," she said, remembering the battered sentry. She rushed to his side and rolled him on his back. Blood oozed through his hair.

"Oh, you poor dear," she said, inspecting the gash on his scalp. Already a welt was rising from the wound. She pried the cork from his canteen.

"This will sting," she said, "but it will cleanse the sore."

He winced as she poured rum into the cut.

"Now drink," she urged him, holding the canteen to his lips. His eyelids fluttered. With a groan he reached a hand to his head.

"Don't touch it," she said. "You will only make it worse. Have you anything to fashion a bandage?"

"In my rucksack."

"I will fetch it. Lie still."

"God bless you, lass."

The sentry opened his eyes. Rachel returned a reassuring smile. His jaw dropped, and he unleashed a horrified scream.

"The ghost," he yelled. "Regina Silsby."

His howls so startled her that she fell backward. Boots and horses' hooves sounded in the city streets, forcing her into the shadows. How would she escape an approaching flood of townsfolk? A lone man or two she might frighten, but an entire mob?

Behind a post of the gallows she huddled, uncertain which direction to flee. Thick fog rolled across the mud flats, enshrouding the shore in gray mist. The haze swallowed the graveyard, the roadway, and finally the gallows itself. As the gloom engulfed her, she wondered, "Why run?" She was exactly where she intended to be, on Boston Neck, flanked by soft mud flats. But for the screaming gate guard and the approaching mob, her scheme was unfolding nicely.

She fought back her fear and tramped the highway toward the mainland. At the narrowest stretch of the Neck, where the mire licked the very fringe of the road, she set down her rucksack and extracted several bundles of kindling wood and straw. After spreading the fuels across the roadway, she soaked them with whale oil.

"Hallo, gate there! What's the shouting about?"

Mounted soldiers approached the archway, followed by a horse team drawing a wagon. Curious citizens trailed the train, their torches glowing in the fog. Capt. Dudley halted at the tunnel.

"Sentry, look alive, man," he said. "On your feet. You'll have a dozen lashes for sleeping on duty."

"Regina Silsby," said the fallen guard. "She was here."

"The ghost? You don't say. Where is she now?"

"She struck me."

Regina Silsby's name rippled through the crowd.

"We heard musketry," said one man. "A shot was fired."

"At the ghost, I'll wager," said another.

"Well, where is she?" said a toothless old man. "Where is this ghost, Regina Silsby?"

"Get you all to your houses," Dudley said, "and be quick about it. Hodges, let's have a look."

He urged his horse through the arch, and the sergeant's mount plodded after him.

"Fog's getting thicker, my lord," Hodges said. "A'fore long we won't be able to see a blessed thing."

"Check those gibbets," Dudley said, indicating the iron cages. Hodges dismounted and drew his cutlass while Dudley watched from his saddle. The sergeant poked about the cages, stumbling on the uneven turf.

"Nothing here, my lord," he said.

"What of the gallows?"

He crossed the road and circled the scaffold.

"All clear, my lord."

"Corporal, bring the wagon forward," Dudley said. "And send those people away."

"To your homes," the corporal said. "Be gone, all of you. Forward, you louts. Lively now."

The wagon rumbled through the archway, and the remaining horsemen followed.

"Hold," Dudley said, raising a hand. "Hodges, did you hear that? You men, fan out. Sweep the graveyard. You others, search the field behind the gibbets. If anyone is hiding there, we'll flush him out."

"The ground's soft, my lord," Hodges said, "and the fog's thick. 'Twould be better if we kept to the highway."

"Do as I say, or I'll see you horsewhipped."

"Aye, my lord. Ho, men, you heard the captain. Sweep the graveyard and behind the gibbets."

Riders and mounts were soon swallowed in mist. Great sucking sounds filled the haze as the animals' hooves sank into the soft earth.

"Mind where you're guiding that beast, Stillwell," said a soldier in the fog. "Treading the graves of lost souls is how Malone's troubles started."

"We'll find worse than Regina Silsby here. Unholy ground, this is, not like the King's Chapel. Every bloody ghost in Boston will be hounding us."

"Left flank, hold your tongues," Dudley said. "Stay alongside. You're falling behind."

"The ground's soft, my lord."

Fire erupted on the roadway, searing the horses' snouts. Inside the blaze hovered the phantom, arms flailing at the animals. Hodges' steed reared and threw him from the saddle. He struck the road and lay still. The wagon veered off the lane and splattered into the muck.

A wheel broke off.

"Load your weapons," Dudley said, struggling to control his stallion.

"My lord, she's gone."

Dudley gaped at the fiery wall. The phantom had vanished.

"Hodges, get up," he said. "Blast you for a beggar's bride. Stillwell, Grady. Find her. She mustn't escape."

Already the flames were dwindling to tiny tongues of fire.

"Bring a rope," said the wagon master from the mud flats. "Get these nags back to the highway."

"Quiet," Dudley said. "She's close by. I can smell her."

His next order stuck in his throat. At his knee floated a grisly face. It shriveled skin wrapped a mouth of black rot, and two demonic eyes glowered at him from tattered sockets. Before he could recover his senses the phantom cupped bony hands beneath his stirrup and heaved upward. Dudley spilled from his saddle and slammed to the ground. His pistol blasted a hole through his coat tail. As the stallion reared, the ghoul vaulted onto his back.

"Fly, beast," she screamed, whipping the animal's flank. Horse and rider bounded toward Boston Gate. A soldier leveled his musket at the fleeing goblin.

"Don't," shouted the corporal. "Mind the crowd."

He swatted the musket upward as it exploded. The bullet ricocheted off the gate's brick wall. Fiendish laughter echoed through the tunnel as the phantom thundered through the archway.

"Saints alive, she's real," said an onlooker.

The crowd scattered. Torches dropped to the pavement and snuffed out. As quickly as she had appeared, the ghost was gone.

"God preserve us," a woman said.

Through the Boston streets Rachel galloped, cackling with devilish laughter. Windows and doors opened as she passed, and the inhabitants gaped at her horrid face. She cared not who saw her. Each witness would embellish the tale.

On a whim she steered the stallion toward the King's Chapel. Leaving the captain's mount in the cemetery would be a brilliant finale to her escapade. Up the hill she raced, the horse's hooves clattering on the cobbles. She urged the stallion to leap the graveyard fence and guided him through the tombstones. At Regina Silsby's grave she dismounted and brushed aside the snow covering the sod. There she left him, munching the exposed grass, to be discovered on the morrow.

At the cemetery's back gate she pulled off her mask and wig and stuffed them into her sack. She climbed the iron bars and dropped to the pavement beyond. Once more the demon ghost of Regina Silsby was the demure daughter of Jeremiah Winslow. She hurried down the hill toward home.

Snow was falling thickly. As she shuffled along she detected a stench of foul leather clinging to her. She paused to wash at a rain barrel in her father's garden. With a fist she shattered the surface ice, then splashed frigid water on her face and throat. The chill sent shudders down her spine. Still dripping, she circled to the back of the house and climbed the woodpile beneath her window.

"Rachel," came a sharp voice from above. Her grandfather was peering at her from his chamber.

"What in heaven's name are you doing?" he said.

"I . . . needed firewood," she said, hoping he would over-look the knotted bed sheet hanging from her window. "I came out for some and . . . the door latched behind me. It is so late, and I wished not to disturb anyone. I thought to climb the woodpile to my room."

"You'll break your neck," he said. "Let me come down for you."

He banged shut his sash, and Rachel met him at the back door.

"Hurry in with you now," he said. "Quite a start you gave me."

"As you gave me," she said. "Mercy, Grandfather, I nearly fainted with fright. And it is so cold tonight. But I'm safe inside now and ready to go abed."

"Are you not forgetting something?" he said.

"What is that?"

"Your firewood."

"Aye, of course. Thank you, Grandfather. I'd have found myself making a second trip."

She trotted back to the woodpile and gathered several pieces in her arms. Her mask dropped into the snow.

"Mercy," she said, and quickly spilled her armload on top of it.

"Don't carry so many," he said. "Two or three should last you 'til morning."

She bent over and scooped up the leather with the wood.

"Thank you so much, Grandfather," she said, planting a kiss on his grizzled cheek as she slipped past him.

"Inside with you now, child," he said. "Get you straight to bed. You'll catch your death of cold."

"Aye, Grandfather. Straight away."

He followed her upstairs and bid her good night from his chamber doorway. After she had disappeared into her room, he stared at the muddy tracks trailing down the hall.

"The missus won't be liking that," he said, shaking his head. He plodded downstairs, found a rag, and wiped the floor.

Eight

✤

Rebuke

"Idiot," Col. Leslie roared. "Imbecile."

He sat at a writing desk in a small office of the Customs House. Capt. Dudley stood stiffly before him.

"Explain to me," Leslie said, "how a king's officer can be bested by a vapor."

"We have witnesses," Dudley said.

"Aye," Leslie said, "four dozen Bostonians who will testify to your complete and utter incompetence."

"That is not what I meant, my lord."

"Hang what you meant. Twice now you have managed to humiliate yourself and a platoon of the king's soldiers. And what's your excuse? A goblin jumped in front of you."

"Regina Silsby is not a ghost, my lord. She—that is to say, he—is a man, like your lordship and myself."

"A man like me he may be, but a man like you he is certainly not."

"I meant that he is flesh and blood, my lord, not a spirit."

"Captain, you have a remarkable flare for the obvious. Of course he's a man. All these cursed Sons of Liberty go romping about dressed as red Indians. Why shouldn't one garb himself as a ghost? But I cannot understand how one buffoon wearing a costume can outwit six armed soldiers and their commanding officer."

"I will catch him, my lord."

"That is what you said yesterday. And this morning Regina Silsby's reputation is rising like that sun out there. Half of Boston claims to have seen her galloping about last night, and today we learn that she was riding your horse. Do you know that at this very moment the entire congregation of King's Chapel is storming the vicar's residence?"

"My lord?"

"They are demanding Regina Silsby's ghost be exorcized from the chapel grounds. There is even talk of digging up her remains and moving them to unconsecrated earth. But no one's willing to do it, because they're all afraid she'll put a curse on them."

"Utter nonsense, my lord."

"Blast you for your stupidity. Real or not, that *ghost* will be blamed for every illness and malady infecting Boston from now on. I've got a bloody panic on my hands. What's worse, the entire 64th regiment is afraid to step outside after dark. All because of your grand performances at the Green Dragon and Boston Neck. And I have not even begun to discuss the gunpowder at Pembroke."

"I have a plan, my lord."

"Dash your plan. By now the powder is not there."

"Of course not, my lord. I shall learn its location. As for this Regina Silsby fellow, I promise your lordship that I shall have the wretch hanging from a gallows."

"If the wretch doesn't wrap a noose around your neck first. One more failure, Capt. Dudley, and you'll be sailing back to England as a cabin boy on a dispatch boat."

"I beg permission, my lord, to hunt down this Regina Silsby and—"

"You beg permission? My dear boy, I am demanding it of you. Find that devil and drag his hide in here. Kill him first, if you must, but I want this nonsense stopped. Do you understand?"

"Perfectly, my lord."

"Good. Now get out of my sight. Don't show your face to me again until you have that scoundrel in irons."

"As you wish, my lord."

Dudley retreated from the colonel's office and closed the door. In the rotunda stood a dozen junior officers mutely watching. Dudley straightened his jacket, squashed his hat on his head and stomped across the marble floor. Whispered conversations trailed him.

"Wipe that smirk from your face," he shouted at a young lieutenant.

"Begging your pardon, my lord," the lieutenant said, saluting. "I wasn't smiling."

"You were."

"Not at all, my lord."

"You think me a coward, don't you?"

"Certainly not, my lord. We were just saying . . ."

"What?"

"Nothing, my lord, nothing at all."

"Liar. Who among you doubts my courage? Speak."

The officers avoided his gaze.

"Peasants," Dudley said. "You are not fit to wear the king's uniform."

He pushed through the outer door and clambered down the stone steps. Into the bustling crowd he tramped, ignoring the men and women he jostled. Abruptly he halted, turned about, and stomped in the opposite direction. Through the maze of streets he marched to Josiah Sinquin's shop. He thrust open the door, jangling the bell on the lintel.

"Jeweler," he said. Robert Winslow bolted from his chair.

"You, boy, where is your master?" Dudley said.

"He is not here, my lord."

"Do you think me blind? I can see he's not here. Where is he? When do you expect him back?"

"I could not say, my lord."

"Blast."

Dudley paced the shop.

"Have you pen and paper?" he said. "I'll leave a message."

"Of course, my lord."

Robert offered the captain quill and paper from Sinquin's writing desk and popped open the tin of ink. Dudley dipped the quill and scratched a note across the sheet. After sprinkling powder on his scribbling, he blew dry the ink and dumped the excess powder on the floor.

"Wax," he said. Robert produced a stick of sealing wax. Dudley lit the taper from a nearby candle and dribbled molten drops across the folded paper.

"See that your master gets this the moment he returns," Dudley said, pressing his ring into the soft wax. He handed the note to Robert.

"Certainly, my lord. Thank you, my lord."

The captain retreated to the street and banged shut the door, leaving Robert to contemplate the sealed note. His lordship must be courting a lady of notable stature, Robert decided. Clearly he was in swift need of a necklace, a bracelet, or a similar token. His urgency would demand a premium price, as usual. Robert wondered if he could read the name of the lady. By squeezing the letter's corners he might manage to peak through its open sides.

He hesitated. To tamper with his master's correspondence was to invite a lashing. But Sinquin rarely returned to his shop before luncheon, and Robert would require only a few seconds to satisfy his curiosity. He studied the letter, turning it over in his hands. His lordship's work had been hasty. The seal was weak, and seemed in danger of popping loose. Robert squeezed the corners of the letter slightly, testing it. The seal sprang free.

Terror seized him. He must restore the seal immediately, or face Sinquin's wrath. As he groped to find the lost seal his curiosity got the better of him. Why not read the letter first? It had opened accidentally, and he could not blame himself for that. Besides, Sinquin never communicated anything to him. Always his master retired to the back room when conversations with his patrons grew serious. Their hushed words fueled in Robert a burning inquisitiveness, but he dared not press an ear to the door, lest his master suddenly emerge and catch him spying. Instead Robert busied himself about the shop, observing everything, learning nothing. How grand it would be to know one of his master's secrets.

With trembling hands he unfolded the paper. His face was hot and flushed, his heart thumping with excitement. As he scanned the letter his cheeks paled. A knot wrung his bowels, and his breakfast squeezed into his throat. He swallowed hard, forcing the bile back into his belly. Dizziness spun his head. The letter slipped from his grasp and floated to the floor.

Suddenly the jeweler's shop seemed a demon's lair. The tools, the tables, the bellows, the brazier, the crucible—all became hellish instruments of evil, and Robert a destitute soul lost in perdition. Escape became his only thought, but to flee would bring a beating.

The letter. He must reseal the letter. That, at least, would cover his transgression. Robert stumbled to the floor and found the paper and seal. He lit the taper and dripped fresh wax on the letter's fold, then fixed the captain's wax disc to it. Once the seal was firm, he laid the letter on Sinquin's desk.

Nine

※

The Press Gang

Rachel stood in a dark corner of her father's barn. Earthy aromas perfumed the air, and morning light filtered through cracks in the planked walls. The cows were munching, the sheep bleating, the pigs slopping, and the chickens brooding. Two geese pecked at kernels of corn scattered over the dirt floor. The dog lay by a fire beneath the laundry cauldron, where a week's worth of wash simmered in scented water.

A single lantern brightened the crossed beams behind the barn door. For the hundredth time that morning she fixed her gaze on the joint where the timbers met. She snatched her letter opener from her skirt and slung it at the beams. It stabbed into the wood, shivering—another perfect throw.

She shuffled to the door and tugged free the blade. Once more she paused to stir the laundry and to check the cranberry stain on her mother's blouse. The smudge was slowly working its way from the fabric. She returned to the far wall and positioned herself with her back to the beams. After a deep breath she spun on her heel and let fly the letter opener once more. Again the blade split the center of the crossbeam.

Weeks before she had measured the barn at twenty paces, and after much exercise she could place the weapon inside a six-inch target from that distance. Whether the mark was before her, behind her or beside her, she could strike it with overhand, underhand, and cross-hand throws.

"How I wish I could show Robert up," she said, flicking the letter opener into the post. Christmas and Epiphany had faded into frigid January's doldrums, with howling winds pummeling the landscape and thick snows smothering everything. All Boston was buttoned up or battened down, and she found herself wondering why she bothered to practice. Her brother was right. What use was knife throwing to a girl? Did it matter that she could split a turnip from across the kitchen? Would she entertain dinner guests with a quick cast through the heart of a minced tart?

"Meaningless," she said, quoting King Solomon. "Everything is useless and chasing after wind."

Still, the exercise was fun, even if it was futile. She sighed and returned to her chores: another log on the fire, another turn of the stirring staff through the laundry, another inspection of the blouse. A month had passed since the ghost had shown herself, and still every tongue in Boston continued to wag about her. Rachel wondered what the fuss was about. Anyone familiar with the Scriptures would know that Regina Silsby could not be a spirit. Holy Writ clearly stated that man was appointed once to die, and after that was his judgment before God. Jesus himself had spoken of a great gulf separating heaven from earth, so that those in one realm could not pass into the other. The only spirits wandering the earth were those cast out of heaven: fallen angels destined for damnation. And Scripture warned that they could appear as angels of light.

"Familiar spirits," she said, thinking of Madame Slocum. Didn't the old woman realize there was only one Holy Spirit, and that all others were unholy spirits? No one would ever learn any truth of the afterlife from them. Liars they were, bent on deceiving gullible souls.

The barn door flung open. Peter Slater stood wild-eyed before her.

"Hide me," he said.

"Peter," she said, "what in heaven's name are you doing here?"

"Confound you, girl, don't ask stupid questions. Hide me."

He clambered up the ladder toward the hay loft.

"Peter Slater," she said, grabbing his ankle. "Get you down from there at once. Are you mad?"

"Stand back," he said, swatting away her hand. She drew back, stunned.

"Peter, what is wrong?"

Before he could answer, three Royal Marines burst into the barn.

"There he is," shouted a corporal. The marines shoved her aside and seized him. Peter struggled to free himself. One man raised his musket and battered the boy's brow. He dropped to the ground, blood streaming from his face.

"How dare you," Rachel said.

"Hold your tongue, lass," the corporal said, "or you'll get as much. Fetch him outside."

She followed as the marines dragged Peter to the stable yard. In the road stood old Mr. Gray, the boy's master, leaning on his walking stick and jabbering at the marines' lieutenant.

"You've no right to do this," Gray was saying. "He's a good lad, he is, and contracted to me for another four years yet."

"On your feet," the lieutenant said, slapping Peter with the flat of his sword. The marines bound his hands and tethered him to a string of despondent youths in the roadway. Some were beaten and bloodied, others simply quaking with dread. One, a mere child, bawled huge tears while his mother pleaded for his release. The lieutenant ignored her and counted his captives.

"Two more," he said. His marines fanned into the streets, leaving three to stand guard.

"I insist you release this lad into my custody," Gray told the lieutenant.

"Off with you, old man," the lieutenant said, "before I have you flogged."

"What goes on here?" said a voice from the house. Capt. Dudley was marching across the stable yard in his shirt sleeves.

"My lord," the lieutenant said with a bow, "this fellow demands that I release that lad yonder."

"The boy's my apprentice," Gray said to Dudley. "He helps me fashion cordage for all his majesty's ships. Already he gives valuable service to the Royal Navy. I cannot work without him. You must tell this man to return him to me."

"I am under orders," the lieutenant said. "Ten able-bodied men are to be taken aboard the *Devonshire* straightaway. Only this morning we lost four to pneumonia."

"But, sir," sobbed the child's mother, "my son is a mere babe. Surely he will be useless on a man-of-war."

"I am in need of a cabin boy," the lieutenant said.

"For the love of God, sir," she said. "Would you steal my only child from me?"

"If you expect some sort of compensation, you may address the matter to Capt. Madden aboard the *Devonshire*."

"Compensation?" Gray said. "How do you compensate for a son?"

"Every man and boy aboard the *Devonshire* is son to someone," the lieutenant said.

"My lord," said the mother, falling before Dudley, "I beg you, on your own mother's heart and soul. Take pity on me. Tell this man to spare my child."

"I'll not have my orders altered for mere sentiment," said the lieutenant. "Surely my lord the captain understands that his majesty's officers must expect compliance in these matters. I daresay the king's loyal subjects should show gratitude for his majesty's protection, by offering whatever service may be required of them."

"Service?" Gray said. "When did robbery and kidnapping become a service to the crown?"

"My actions are entirely legal," said the lieutenant. "I am imposing on you no harsher duty than would be expected of any Englishman."

"Englishmen we may be," Gray said, "but we are American Englishmen, with our own laws and our own magistrates."

"And your own king?" the lieutenant said. "Guard your tongue, old man, for that is rebel talk."

"I am no more a rebel than you," Gray said. "I served in the king's regiments and was decorated for it."

He turned to Dudley and said, "My lord, tell this lieutenant to cease his outrages. We are not slaves or chattel, but Englishmen, same as he."

"I am in no position to countermand the lieutenant," Dudley said. "The king's agents have every right to exercise his majesty's sovereignty over his subjects. You'll have to find yourself another apprentice."

"What of this poor woman? Will she find another son for herself?"

Dudley gazed down his nose at her.

"Let her bear another," he said.

"The devil take you," Gray said, his walking stick quaking in his fist. "Have you no heart or decency about you? Steal my apprentice from me, if you must, but can you not release this woman's only child to her?"

"If she has a complaint," Dudley said, "she may take it to Captain Madden aboard the *Devonshire*."

"Hang Captain Madden. Hang the lot of you. No wonder you've so many Sons of Liberty springing up about you. Scoundrels, that's what you are. You pillage and plunder like so many buccaneers, all in the name of his majesty's sovereign rights."

"How dare you speak to me thus."

"I shall speak to you any way I please," Gray said. "Your thievery may serve you well in England, but you'll find little tolerance for it here."

"I must warn you of your insolence, sir."

"And I defy you your arrogance, sir. If a man steals thrice, he is hanged for a common criminal, and rightly so. But when you steal ten children from their homes, do you expect us to thank you for his majesty's protection? Fie on his majesty's protection. And fie on you, for inflicting it upon us."

"I'll hear no more of this," Dudley said.

"Indeed you will not."

Gray raised his walking stick and struck Dudley behind the ear.

"Marines," said the lieutenant. "Arrest that man."

The guards seized him.

"My lord, are you hurt?" the lieutenant said.

"Of course not," Dudley said, brushing his shoulder where the blow had fallen.

"Twelve lashes for that one," the lieutenant said. "Take him to the pillory by the Customs House."

Rachel stepped forward.

"Sir," she said, "please allow my protest. Mr. Gray is old and feeble. Twelve lashes might well kill him."

"He should have considered that before he struck a king's officer."

"I'll take their lashes," Gray said, "be they twelve or twenty. You tempt me to join the Sons of Liberty myself."

"Enough of this nonsense," Dudley said. "My dear lieutenant, for the sake of the young lady I would be lenient. You needn't flog the old fool on my account."

"My lord is too generous."

"It is a fault, I admit."

"Three days in the pillory, then," the lieutenant said.

"But sir," Rachel said, "that is no better. Three days in this foul weather would finish him."

"Three days," the lieutenant said. "Now take him away. Marines, fetch these dogs to the long boat. I'll send a cutter for the others."

The marines lashed Gray's wrists and marched him down the street with the other captives.

"My lord," Rachel said to Dudley, "you cannot allow this sentence to be carried out."

"He struck a king's officer," Dudley said. "That I cannot undo."

"The punishment hardly fits the offense."

"In this case I must agree with you. The penalty for assaulting a king's officer is death. Under the circumstances, the old man should be grateful for a sporting chance to have his life."

"He shall certainly freeze, my lord."

"With a blanket on his back and a bowl of hot soup in his belly, he may make a go of it. What say you? I'll wager two guineas he lives to tell this tale."

"I say my lord values the lives of those he protects but little."

"Watch your tongue, lass. I've done more for him, and for you, than most."

"Who shall provide the soup?" she said.

"You tell me," Dudley said. "How much do *you* value his life?"

He strutted toward the house. She watched him go, then stomped to the barn and slammed shut the door.

"Insolent," she said, fuming as she paced back and forth. What unspeakable arrogance. Who were these men, that they regarded the lives of others so disdainfully? How could they ignore God's truth that all men were equal before Him? Did they really think themselves superior beings because of their haughty titles and gaudy uniforms?

Suddenly she stopped. Scattered thoughts tumbling in her mind crystallized into a revelation. Samuel Adams was right. The king's soldiers were a menace; the king's agents were a menace. And because they merely reflected the attitude of their sovereign, the king himself was the true menace. His majesty considered his subjects mere cattle, to be taxed, and yoked, and beaten, and butchered as whim carried him. It was intolerable, it was unspeakable, it was . . .

"Tyranny," she said aloud.

In God's kingdom, the greatest were servants of all. And should not God's people reflect His realm on earth? If the king were truly a servant of God, would he not consider himself a servant to his subjects, rather than the other way around? Would not the king's agents reflect their master's attitude in manner and bearing? By their arrogance they showed themselves servants of their true master, the devil, and their true master's bidding is what they did.

Her eyes fell on the letter opener, still protruding from the crossbeams behind the door. An Old Testament proverb silenced all other thoughts in her head.

"If thou forbear to deliver them that are drawn unto death, and those that are ready to be slain; if thou sayest, Behold, we knew it not; doth not he that pondereth the heart consider it? and he that keepeth thy soul, doth he not know it? and shall not he render to every man according to his works?"

"Impossible," she said aloud, shaking away the voice. What hope had a single, costumed clown against a warship packed stem-to-stern with fighting men? Only a fool would consider such an errand. The previous month she had been stupid enough to visit Boston Neck without the Lord's blessing; she would certainly not venture aboard the *Devonshire* apart from Him now.

She doused the laundry fire, wrung out the garments, and hung them to dry on the rafters.

"I shall bring Mr. Gray some stew," she said as she crossed the garden to the kitchen. "Beyond that, I can do nothing." But the proverb continued to badger her brain.

If I pretend to know nothing about it . . .

"But I'm not pretending," she said aloud.

. . . will He not repay me according to what I do, or do not do?

"I'm one girl," she said. "How many men are aboard the *Devonshire?* Seven hundred? It is madness."

She thought, "But at night they will be sleeping."

"Not enough of them," she said. "There will be sentries and watches posted. The very idea is preposterous. How can I brave Boston harbor alone and . . ."

The complaint died on her lips. Neighbors were staring at her across the garden fence.

"Are you ill, lass?" one said. "Who is it you're talking to?"

"No one," she said, "no one at all."

She retreated to the house. In the kitchen Grandfather was sharpening a knife by the hearth.

"Have you taken ill?" he said. "You're all red and flushed."

"I'm off to the Customs House," she said. "They've taken Mr. Gray to the pillory."

With a ladle she sampled the thick stew simmering in the cauldron.

"The rope maker?" he said. "Whatever for?"

"Royal Marines have pressed his apprentice into service," she said. "Mr. Gray tried to stop them."

Grandfather gaped at her.

"A press gang is roaming Boston?" he said.

"With my own eyes I saw them," she said. "They came into our barn. Peter Slater and nine others have been taken aboard the *Devonshire*."

He laid the knife in his lap.

"I cannot recall ever seeing a press gang in America," he said.

"You may soon see more of them."

She filled a bowl with meaty broth and cradled it in a basket.

"How long is Gray's sentence?" he said.

"Three days. He struck Capt. Dudley with his cane."

"Did he? The swaggerer probably deserved it. But old Gray'll die before three days are done."

"I am taking some stew to him," she said. "Perhaps that will help."

"He'll want more than a bowl of beef to stay alive."

"There's not much else we can do."

He nodded, and said, *"Man is born unto trouble, as the sparks fly upward."*

"I beg your pardon?"

" 'Tis a verse, lass, from the book of Job. Shall I tell your mother where you've gone?"

"Please."

With the basket on her arm, a bread loaf in her hand, and a blanket over her shoulder, she marched to the Customs House. The plight of the prophet Jonah came to mind. God had ordered him to Nineveh, and Jonah had refused to go. He had ended up in a whale's belly. After the huge fish had spit him onto shore, Jonah still had to journey to Nineveh. Rachel always thought Jonah would have had a simpler time of it had he obeyed at the first. Now she understood why he had not. By his troubles the prophet had learned that no place was safe outside of the Lord's will.

On a raised platform before the Customs House stood the public pillory. Soldiers were strapping Gray's head and hands into the holed planks. A sergeant then fastened down the boards with chain and padlock. Sullen citizens watched from the street below.

Rachel crossed the square and mounted the scaffold.

"Mr. Gray," she said, pushing past the sergeant, "I have brought some stew for you."

"Rachel Winslow," the old man said, craning his neck for a glimpse of her. "God bless you, lass. I'll not let the good Lord forget your kindness."

"Quiet, there," said the sergeant while pocketing his key ring. "You, lass, state your business."

"I have brought a meal for Mr. Gray," she said.

"Hurry on, then. Fill him up and be off with you."

She spooned stew to Gray's lips and noticed onlookers watching from the street.

"Has any of you a spare blanket?" she said. "Mine alone will hardly keep him warm."

"Let the Tory freeze," said one man. He turned and tramped away. Others grumbled their assent.

"Whether you agree with his politics or not," she said, "the Lord instructed us to love our neighbors as ourselves. Did He not say, 'I was in prison, and ye came unto me'? Have any of you a kindness to render this man on behalf of your Lord and Master?"

The crowd dispersed, wagging their heads.

"He hasn't many friends in that lot," said the sergeant. "Get along, lass. I've yet to taste my own supper."

Gray gobbled his stew as best he could, and after it was gone she fed him the bread loaf. He was finishing the final scraps when two women appeared at the scaffold stair.

"I've brought my footwarmer from church," said one, showing Rachel the metal box. "There's two oven-hot bricks inside, and I'll bring you two more on the morrow."

"Thank you," Rachel said. The woman's companion draped a thick woolen blanket over Gray's shoulders.

"This will warm him right enough," she said. " 'Twas my own mother's, and I never felt a cold night beneath it."

"God bless you, madame," Gray said. "Don't you fret yourself a wee bit about me. I've been in worse straits than this and came out better for them."

"Very well, then," the sergeant said. "Off with you now, until the morrow."

Rachel followed the other ladies down the scaffold steps.

"A word fitly spoken is like apples of gold in pictures of silver."

She paused, suddenly alert. Why had that verse from Solomon's proverbs popped into her brain? As the sergeant pushed past her the puzzle became a plan, a plan that would require many words.

"My thanks to you, good sergeant," she said, hurrying to his side as he tramped toward the Customs House. "I shall bring Mr. Gray a warm breakfast on the morrow, and a good supper too. He's a fine fellow, Mr. Gray is, once you get to know him. I'll grant you he seems a bit gruff at times, especially now, with his head and hands all trussed up in the pillory like that. Humiliating, don't you agree? I should think it enough to put anyone in a dark mood. But he's a soft heart, Mr. Gray has, really. Perhaps you'll come to consider him a father. I'm sure I do—or perhaps a grandfather would be more appropriate. He's a bit old to be a father to me, isn't he? But you, perhaps . . ."

Up the Custom House steps and through the large doors she followed him, jabbering all the way.

" 'Twill be a cold night," she said as they passed beneath the domed ceiling. "I can't remember the weather ever being so cold as this."

He ignored her and entered a tiny office. She followed him through the door.

"Would you believe," she said, "this is Mr. Gray's first offense in his life? Imagine that. The poor dear must be up-wards of seven-and-sixty years if he's a day. He served with the king's grenadiers against the French and Indians, you know. Did you fight in that war? No, I suppose not. All that time, and not a single—"

"Woman," he said, "cease your pointless chatter this in-stant."

He dropped onto a stool before a small writing desk.

"Oh, I do beg your pardon, sir," she said. "I shall be quiet at once. Aye, sir, by your command. Gracious, I know not what's come over me. Perhaps it is Mr. Gray's trouble that has put me out of sorts. The last time I found myself babbling so much was two summers ago, when my cousins came up from Philadelphia and—"

"If you've any business here," he said, "state it and be gone. Better yet, just be gone."

He reached into his waistcoat and dropped his key ring into the desk drawer. She noted the spot and the window on the far wall.

"I meant no offense, sir," she said with a curtsy. "I've really no business at all, except to ask that you'll check on Mr. Gray from time to time during the night, and make sure he's—"

"Get you gone," he said. "Out, I say, at once."

"Aye, sir. Right away, sir. You've been too kind. I shall be off immediately, and trouble you no further."

Ten

Rescue

"Ten o'clock and all's well," said the night watchman. A tolling church bell confirmed his report, and distant chimes echoed the steady drone. Four soldiers paced the perimeter of the Customs House square, muskets protruding from the blankets on their backs. Scattered snowflakes were thickening into swirls as the watchman strolled the cobbles to the scaffold.

"How fare you, Mr. Gray?" he said.

"Well enough," Gray said through chattering teeth. "My footwarmer's grown cold."

" 'Twill be a bitter night," the watchman said with a glance at the sky. "I shall return at half-past. Perhaps the tavern yonder will give us a warm brick or two."

He departed into the shadows and sidestepped one of the sentries.

"He'll not live to see dawn," the guard said.

"I think he has enough spirit in him," the watchman said.

"One night's worth, perhaps, but three?"

"We will have to wait and see."

Neither man noticed a dark phantom crouched in the shadows behind them. Had the ghoul stretched forth a bony hand, she could have touched the watchman as he passed from the square. Instead her eyes followed him down the street, then returned to the soldiers.

Falling snow obscured houses and trees. The ghost checked the fit of her mask and wig, pausing as two guards crossed in front of her hiding place.

"What say you now, Jones?" said one. "With these snows tumbling down, even you must agree he'll be gone by midnight."

"Rain's worse than snow," Jones said. "He'll see daylight right enough. 'Twill be tomorrow night that kills him."

"Will you wager on that?"

"A pint of ale?"

"Make it two."

"Done."

The soldiers strolled by the Red Flagon tavern, and the ghost fell in behind them. Past the walls of brick and board she drifted, her steps silenced by the deepening carpet of snow. At the Customs House she vanished into a side street and appeared minutes later on one of the building's columned porticos. At a window on the far wall she halted, hovering in the shadow of a tall pillar.

Rachel stood before the window quietly counting the seconds—fifty-eight, fifty-nine, sixty, making eight minutes. One, two, three . . .

It was a dull chore, but profoundly necessary. Icy flakes gathered on her hood and shoulders. Not until the twelfth minute did she move, reaching into a pocket to extract a large rock.

"Thirty-two, thirty-three, thirty-four," she counted, afraid she might be rushing her tempo. She pressed a hand to the window and peered through the glass. Somewhere in that darkness was the sergeant's writing desk, and in its drawer lay the key to the pillory.

A sentry paced the lane at the bottom of the marble steps, adjusting his blanket against the worsening chill. At the fourteenth minute Rachel raised her rock to the window.

"Twenty-six, twenty-seven, twenty-eight . . ."

The church bell struck quarter-past. She punched her stone through the pane. Glass shattered, spraying shards across the wooden floor inside. She extracted her arm from the hole and glanced up the street. Echoes of the church bell died away. A carriage rolled across the square. Sentries wandered past. No one ventured onto the Customs House portico. She reached through the broken pane and unlatched the window. After lifting the sash, she shook the snow from her cloak and slipped through the opening.

The room was warm and dry. Red coals glowed in a corner hearth, and by their feeble light she discerned a misshapen lump on the floor. Snores reverberated from it. Beyond the slumbering soldier was the writing desk, and beside it stood a chair strewn with clutter. The door on the far wall was closed.

She decided the guard's feet were too close to the wall to allow her safe passage. The longer path around his head would have to serve. She eased a foot forward and shifted her weight to it. Glass crunched beneath her boot. The sleeping man snorted. He rolled beneath his blanket, mumbled something and adjusted the wool about his chin. Several sniffles were followed by a cough and a clearing of the throat. Eventually the snores resumed their former rhythm.

Cautiously she advanced a step, then another. Her skirts brushed the soldier's blanket. He stirred. She bent over, gathered her dress about her ankles, and slowly rounded his head. If he had chosen that moment to open his eyes he would have been staring into the mangled face of Regina Silsby. But he continued to snore, and with a pair of backward steps she eased from him toward the desk. Turning slowly about, she extended her hands toward the desk and wrapped her fingers around the drawer's brass knob. A gentle pull and . . . the drawer was locked.

Is nothing simple? she thought. With her fingers she searched the desk top for some tool that might help her pry open the drawer. Quill pens, an ink bottle and sealing wax littered the writing surface, plus a tin of powder, matchsticks, a candle and snuffer, and a deck of playing cards. Frustrated, she glanced about the room. Among the clutter on the chair was the soldier's rucksack. Perhaps it contained a mess kit, with a fork or spoon. She crept toward the chair. Gradually the heaps crowding it became a canteen and cartridge pouch. At the tail end of a tangled strap hung a sheathed bayonet.

Perfect, she almost said aloud. She slid the steel spike from its scabbard and returned to the desk. By fitting the weapon into the crevice above the keyhole she managed to pop open the drawer. A quick search of its contents unearthed the sergeant's keys. She clutched them firmly to prevent their clattering against each other and buried the entire bundle in a pocket. With the bayonet she forced the drawer back into its locked position, amused at the mystery she was creating. The keys would be discovered in the empty stock's padlock, with no one able to guess how they had gotten there. Doubtless the guard would insist he had been alert inside the room the entire time, leaving no natural explanation for the phenomenon.

" 'Twas the ghost," the soldiers would say, "Regina Silsby."

The bayonet jammed in the drawer. She tugged, but could not loosen the weapon. Back and forth she wriggled it. A grunt escaped her lips. The soldier snorted. She propped a hip against the drawer and heaved. Suddenly the weapon sprang loose. It clattered to the floor and she tumbled backward. Across the chair she fell, and collapsed with it onto the sleeping man's legs.

"Who's there?" he said, recoiling.

She shoved her face against his. The man screamed. She leapt from him and dove through the open window. Across the portico she slid, banging against the column.

"Regina Silsby!" said the terrified soldier. Fists were hammering on the chamber door as she slammed shut the window. She fled down the portico steps as quickly as the slick marble would allow and disappeared into the lane behind the Customs House. At the corner of the building she slipped on the icy pavement and crashed to the ground. Ignoring the pain she picked herself up and hobbled to the square. All four sentries were climbing the snowy steps to the Customs House entry.

"Open," they said, thumping the door with the butts of their muskets. She grabbed her skirts and scurried to the pillory. On the platform Mr. Gray was shivering from head to toe. The blankets had fallen from his back and lay in a heap at his feet. She brushed the snow from his shoulders.

"Who's there?" he said weakly. She realized she must answer, if only to keep him quiet. And if she spoke he might easily recognize her. Forcing her voice into the back of her throat, she said, "Hush. You must be quiet." The words rumbled like the croak of a hoarse toad.

"Who are you?" he said.

"My name does not matter."

She fit a key into the lock. It wouldn't turn.

"What are you doing?" he said.

"Freeing you. Be still."

The sentries continued to pummel the Customs House entry with their muskets. The door splintered, and the sentries collided with soldiers fleeing the building.

"She was here," someone said. "Regina Silsby."

"Dewey says she attacked him—threw a chair across the room."

"Search the building. Find her."

Rachel abandoned the first key and fumbled for the next. It, too, failed. Her fingers were quaking with agitation as she tried the third and fourth keys. Why would none of them work?

Lights began to brighten the windows along the square. She fit the final key into the lock and gave it a sharp twist. With a loud click the hasp popped open.

"Thank God," she said aloud. She yanked the padlock from the stock and left it dangling on its chain, the key still jammed in the keyhole. Throwing back the crossbeam, she grabbed Gray's collar and hauled him from the open portals. He was too stiff to straighten up.

"This way," she said in her toad's voice. She bundled the blanket about his shoulders and urged him down the stairs. Together they fled to a narrow alley. There she halted to survey the activity in the square. Soldiers were pouring from the Customs House, many only half-dressed. Already one man was mounting the empty pillory.

"The prisoner's gone," he said.

"Stolen away," said another, "by Regina Silsby."

Townsfolk appeared in their doorways, still garbed in night gowns and caps. Rachel watched from the alley.

"Go," she said to Gray, "before the soldiers find you."

"Where?" he said. "I cannot return to my house."

She thought a moment, and said, "Get you to the Green Dragon. Tell the innkeeper what has happened. You will find shelter there."

"But my apprentice . . ."

"I will fetch him for you. Flee, while you can."

"Who are you?"

"That is not for you to know."

"You're not a Son of Liberty."

"No."

"Who, then?"

She turned her face to him.

"By my faith," he said, trembling. "Regina Silsby. What do you want of me? I've done nothing to you."

"Silence," she said. "You will bring the entire regiment down on us."

"They say you search for a husband. You've come to carry me to the grave, haven't you?"

"You are too old and ugly for me. Now be off with you. Hurry."

"But why—"

"No more questions. Be gone."

He stared at her cloak and the strips of white cloth stitched to her gloves.

"You are not a spirit," he said.

"Who or what I am is not your affair," she said. "You must go, now. But promise that you'll keep my secret."

"So I shall," he said. "Whoever you are, Regina Silsby, you have saved my life, and may God bless you for it."

She nodded and waved him into the darkness.

"God bless *and* preserve me," she said after he was gone. Soldiers were spreading through the nearby alleys, but in the wrong direction. She retreated to a narrow lane approaching the waterfront. Barely visible in the snowstorm beyond the docks was the British fleet riding at anchor.

"Now for the *Devonshire*," she said.

Eleven

Aboard the Devonshire

Snow tumbled from the night sky, smothering torches and lanterns. British soldiers stampeded through the lanes while nightcapped citizens watched from upper windows. Word passed along the houses that the redcoats sought Regina Silsby. The ghost had visited the Customs House and had stolen away the prisoner in the pillory.

From the wharf Rachel spied a telltale glow of search parties approaching the wharves. She adjusted her mask and descended the stone steps to the water's edge, choosing one of the larger skiffs that bobbed among the pilings. After peeling off the boat's canvas cover and stowing the fabric astern, she climbed aboard and pulled a bundle of rags from a pocket.

Her grandfather had spoken of swaddling oars with cloths to muffle their splashing.

"Sergeant," came a shout from the square. "Search the piers and the counting houses. You there, check the boats."

"Aye, sir. This way, lads, quick march."

Footsteps shuffled toward the water's edge. Rachel wrapped her rags around the blades of the oars, and tied the cloths in place with cords. After releasing the mooring line, she seated herself with her back to the bow and pulled on the oars. The boat slogged through a swell and threatened to wallow among the pilings. Again she heaved on the oars, curling and reaching, her shoulders pressed to her knees one moment and stretched toward the bow the next. She did not bother to mask her grunting, since the soldiers were making more noise than she. The skiff slid away from the pier and was soon clawing toward the open harbor. She glimpsed several soldiers tramping down the stone steps of the wharf. Moments later they were swallowed in swirling white.

Despite the blinding snow, she reasoned the Devonshire would not be difficult to locate. It was one of the largest ships in the fleet—a sixty-four gunner, Grandfather had said. While tugging the oars, she rehearsed in her mind the layout of the ship. More than a year had passed since she had sailed one of her father's packets to the West Indies. Usually she served as assistant to the cook or the quartermaster, and mended sails when necessary. She liked dressing as one of the crew, in a man's shirt and trousers, her long hair knotted at the back of her neck. Her favorite pastime was to go aloft and admire the view from the tops, or to stand at the tip of the bowsprit with nothing in front of her but open ocean, and nothing beneath but foaming waves.

A dark hull loomed in the blizzard ahead of her. Another appeared, followed by still more. Soon she was surrounded by ships. There were single-masted dispatch boats, not much larger than her own, rolling on the waves. Broad-bowed packets, troop transports, and frigates huddled like slumbering wolves. Some vessels were grappled together in twos and threes, others hibernated alone. Through the heart of the dragons' lair she rowed, passing one giant after another until, like a great behemoth emerging from a cave, appeared the towering mass of a line-of-battle ship.

She gasped at the immensity of the vessel. It rose from the water like a colossal sea monster with three masts vanishing into the snowstorm. Ice crusted every spar and line, forming a web of crystal over the black hull. The cabin lights glowed a dim yellow, and a huge flag drooped from the stern, dragging its tip in the water.

Slowly she circled the warship. From the far side of the stern she drew close enough to read the name beneath the cabin windows—*Devonshire*.

Fear gripped her. The task was too great. Even the hardiest adventurer would never board a British man-of-war alone.

There was still time to turn back. She could find an empty wharf, wander home to her bed and curl up in the cocoon of her thick down comforter. By morning the adventure would be only a bad memory. But what of the ten boys trapped in the bowels of that great beast? Could she ever enjoy the ease of her own hearth, knowing that they wallowed in despair?

"Surely there is someone more qualified to this task," she said. A person of ability, skill, and daring would be a far better choice—someone likely to succeed.

She steered her skiff along the ship's side, inching toward the chains amidships. A ladder of stubby wooden planks climbed to the open deck above. Dozens of times, perhaps hundreds, she had made similar climbs while swimming about her father's ships in the tropics. But those were frivolous larks in sun-baked bays, not midnight ascents up icy cliffs of oak. She stowed her oars and tethered the boat to one of the iron rings serving as a handrail.

A final time she arranged her mask. In her pockets were various tools and tricks, and after assuring herself that all were ready, she hauled herself onto the ladder. Her boots slid on the icy planks. The skiff veered away from the ship and left her dangling. She clutched the chains and struggled to find her footing, while snow and ice whirled about her. A large swell rolled the ship, almost plunging her into the frigid water. She pulled her knees to her chest and barely escaped a soaking. The waves plummeted away from her, and she scrambled for a foothold on the ladder. At last she regained her balance and inched upward toward the rail.

The deck was deserted, except for a few officers aft and a sentry forward. All were leaning on the opposite rail, watching the commotion ashore. She pulled herself over the gunwale and dropped between two cannon carriages. Just beyond was a steep stair descending below decks. She hurried toward it and disappeared through the opening.

Not a soul was visible below, but loud snores betrayed the presence of the slumbering crew. Hundreds of men were suspended in hammocks slung from the overhead beams. Back and forth they swayed with every roll of the ship. Great iron guns nuzzled the bulkheads. A marine strolled by. After he had passed she descended to the lower gun deck, and to the storage deck below that. As she expected, the ship's stores were deserted. Casks, crates, and cables crammed the dark space, but not a living being was present to pester her, except the ship's rats and roaches. Quietly, carefully, she made her way forward.

A feeble lamp brightened the ship's cockpit.

"I did do it," said a gravelly voice in the lighted area, "with these very hands I did it."

"Not in your sorry life," came a rough reply. Rachel squeezed between a pair of hogshead casks and peered forward. Two aged mariners were gambling at cards on a sea chest. One was fat and gray and hampered by a wooden leg. His companion seemed more withered than a prune. They were sharing a half-empty bottle of rum and a leg of mutton.

" 'Twas I that cut off old Bender's leg," said the prune, gnawing a chunk of meat and draining his copper mug. "Look here."

He lifted the chest's lid with brittle hands. The bottle dropped to the deck, and the cards scattered.

"Mind what you're doing," said the fat one. Rachel decided by his wooden leg and plump figure that he must be the ship's cook. And the prune was certainly the ship's surgeon.

"This here's the very saw I used on him," the surgeon said, holding aloft a rusty blade with gnarled teeth. "Right above the knee it was, a good clean cut. Rough seas, too—mighty proud of that surgery, I was. He screamed like the bloody devil, but what of it? To this very day he's walking about, wearing as fine a leg of polished ivory as I've ever seen."

"Water," came a feeble voice from a nearby locker. The door was chained shut, but through its wooden grating Rachel recognized Peter Slater's face.

"Pipe down," yelled the cook. "You'll be hanging from a yardarm soon enough, you bilge rat, and I'll not be wasting any water on the likes of you."

He hurled his mug at the locker. Peter clawed at the cup as it banged against the wooden slats. Rum spilled across the deck. The cook laughed and tore another chunk from his mutton leg.

"Please," Peter said.

"I'll teach you to quiet down," the cook said. He grabbed a mallet and staggered toward the locker. Rachel saw her chance. She leapt forward, seized the rum bottle, and clubbed the surgeon with it. The glass shattered, and the surgeon slumped across the open chest.

"Confound you," the cook shouted, pounding the locker door with the mallet, "come out of there, you sorry urchin. I'll have your tongue in my pocket a'fore I've done with you. Where's that saw, Doc?"

He discovered the limp body of the surgeon lying across the trunk.

"So, gone to sleep on me, have you?" he said. "Roast your weak belly. Two drams of rum and you're out like a lubber. Where's that saw?"

On hands and knees he crawled about the deck, searching for the lost instrument. Rachel stepped forward and snatched the mallet from his grasp.

"Here now, give that back," he said, looking up.

She hammered his brow, and he dropped beside his mate. With a gloved hand she grabbed the saw and started toward the lockers, then halted by the trunk. In a shallow tray beneath the surgeon's body lay the finest collection of knives she had never seen. She dragged him aside and scooped up one of the blades.

"Marvelous balance," she said. "I might use one of these."

"Who's there?" Peter Slater said. Quickly she hid her face in her cloak.

"Hush," she said in her toad's voice. She seized every blade in the surgeon's chest and dumped them into a pocket before approaching the locker.

"What are you doing?" Peter said as she sawed one of the grating's slats. Another lad pressed his face to the bars.

"Can't you see?" he said. "She's come to free us. God bless you, woman."

"Silence," Rachel croaked.

"Aye, right enough," the boy said. "But who are you, and how did you get on board? The ship's crawling with Royal Marines."

"My stars," Peter said. " 'Tis the ghost, Regina Silsby. Look at her."

"For heaven's sake," she said. "Why not shout it to the entire ship?"

"You are the ghost, are you not?"

"That is what I am called."

"See here, lads," Peter said, kicking his comrades awake. "Regina Silsby's come to fetch us out."

The boys rubbed their eyes and blinked at her.

"Saints alive," one said.

"Quiet," Peter said. "I see what she's doing. You mean to cut out the window, don't you, Regina Silsby? Have you any more saws? We'll help."

A good idea, she thought. She handed hers to him and dug through the surgeon's chest, finding two more. Eagerly the boys accepted the tools and began carving the slats with them.

It was exasperating work. Rachel stood guard against intruders while the boys took turns exhausting themselves.

"Don't stop now," one would whisper. "Here, let me have a go at it."

"Your turn," another would say, dropping back for a companion to take his place.

"Let's see if she'll give way now," one of the stouter boys decided. With his back to the bulwarks he pressed his feet against the grating. Several kicks could not dislodge the wooden bars.

"Quiet," Rachel said in her toad's voice. "Use the saws to cut some more."

Footsteps clumped on the deck above. Everyone froze. The surgeon groaned. He was awakening. She adjusted her grip on the mallet, ready to strike him another blow. The overhead footsteps wandered away, and the boys resumed their hacking.

"You don't have to saw them all the way through," Peter said. "Just enough to kick them out."

"But that will make too much noise," said another.

"Not if we're careful. There now, that's good enough. William, have another go at it."

The stout boy pressed his feet a second time to the grating, and the wood splintered apart.

"Well done," Peter said. "Come on, lads, through the window here."

One by one the boys squeezed through the opening. Rachel counted nine prisoners.

"There were ten of you," she said. "Who is missing?"

"The youngest," Peter told her. "He's aft, in the officer's mess."

"We must bring him with us."

"It is too dangerous."

"I came for you, did I not?"

"Where will you take us?"

"I've a skiff on the starboard beam," she said. "We'll escape down the chains. Give me that lamp."

Peter slipped the lantern from its iron hook.

"Now listen, all of you," she said. "Keep your wits about you and follow me. Don't make a sound. With luck we'll be away before anyone realizes."

They trailed her to the ladder and climbed unhindered to the upper gun deck.

"Hush," she said, pressing a finger to her lips. "Wait here, between the guns."

She handed her lantern and mallet to Peter and slunk astern. A sliver of light beamed from the closed door of the officer's cabin. Two marines stood beneath the hatch that opened to the quarter deck.

"What's all the fuss ashore about?" one called up the hatch.

"Can't say for certain," came a reply from the upper deck. "There's torches roaming all about the waterfront."

Rachel squeezed between the last gun and the bulwark by the cabin door.

"My lord, you are not serious," said a voice within the cabin.

"I am. In my next dispatch I shall recommend to his majesty's government that the port of Boston be closed. If the prime minister agrees, not a ship will enter or leave Boston until that cursed Tea Party's losses are repaid."

"Is that not unjust, my lord?"

"How so, Lieutenant?"

"If you close the port, will you not punish the innocent along with the guilty?"

"Boston has no innocents, man."

"Many citizens do not share the sentiments of these Sons of Liberty, my lord. Less than three hundred took part in this Tea Party."

"While thousands more watched from the jetties."

"And still more thousands stayed quietly at home. Surely we can round up three hundred miscreants, my lord. But if we close the port, we will starve every man, woman and child in the city."

"You betray your commoner's roots, Lieutenant. Unless you discipline them all, the guilty will go unchastened."

"Surely such sweeping reprisals are not justice, but . . ."

". . . What, Lieutenant? You would be wise to choose your words more carefully."

"The king is not a god, my lord."

"He is to you and me. Really, sir, you tempt me to think you are a rebel yourself."

"Not at all, my lord."

"Then belay such talk and do your duty by him."

"There is news," said another voice, "of other tea parties along the coast, as far south as Virginia. It is becoming epidemic."

"*Fashionable,* these so-called patriots would say."

"The entire country is setting itself ablaze."

"And the best way to stop a fire," said the host, "is to douse it completely before it engulfs everything. By closing the port we'll drown these rebels and their treason."

"Hear, hear."

"Boy! Bring us another plate of beef."

The cabin door opened. Out stepped the child Rachel sought.

"Who goes there?" said one of the marines from the hatchway.

"The captain wants another plate of beef, sir," the boy said.

"Very well, get on with you."

Already the boy's cheeks were purpled by blows. He closed the door while the marines returned their attention to the upper deck. Rachel clapped a hand across the boy's mouth and dragged him into the corner with her. He saw her face and gaped in terror.

"Be not afraid," she whispered in her own voice. "I've come to return you home to your mother. Can you keep silent?"

He nodded. Slowly she removed her hand from his lips.

"Are you the ghost?" he whined.

"I am," she said, stroking his cheek, "and you are a brave lad. Trust me, and all will be well."

She took his hand and scooted with him to the ladder.

"This way," she said in her frog's voice. Peter handed her the lantern and mallet, and she climbed the ladder to the ship's waist. There she came face to face with a Royal Marine. Both gasped.

"The ghost," he shouted. "Alarm, alarm!"

She clubbed him with the mallet. Officers at the rail whirled about.

"Hurry," Rachel said to the boys. "Over the side with you."

They scurried to the open deck.

"Turn out the night watch," an officer said, drawing his sword. "Intruders aboard."

Footsteps pounded below. Hatches crashed open and armed marines swarmed topside.

"Retreat," Rachel told the boys. "To the forecastle."

They clamored toward the bow, stampeding the guard who tried to block them. From her cloak Rachel slipped a bottle of lamp oil. She dashed it on the deck and hurled her lantern into the oil slick. Flames shot upward.

"Fire," the marines shouted. "Fire on deck."

"All hands, man the pumps," said an officer astern. "Fetch the buckets, you dogs."

Rachel fled forward.

"We'll have to jump the rail," she said. "Is there any among you who cannot swim?"

The cabin boy raised his hand.

"Take charge of him," she said, shoving the child into Peter's arms. "See that he gets ashore."

Peter swallowed his fear and nodded. Sailors and marines were spilling across the ship's waist, passing canvas buckets of seawater, and splashing them over the blaze. The flames spread.

"Imbeciles," said an officer. "That's oil burning. Break out the sand casks."

"Where's the ghost?"

"Never mind her. Prepare to flood the magazine."

"There she is at the bows. Marines, form up here. Load your firelocks."

From the stern cabin poured a handful of hatless officers, some with dinner napkins still tucked into their collars. Capt. Dudley stood open mouthed among them.

Sailors pushed past him carrying buckets of sand. Unless they were stopped, they would put out the fire. Rachel dug into her pocket and grabbed the surgeon's knives. Taking aim on the forward-most sand bucket, she hurled a dagger that pinned itself deep into the pail's side. The startled sailor dropped the bucket, scattering its sand. She threw a second dagger, but her aim was bad and the blade buried itself in a sailor's thigh. With a shriek he collapsed, clutching his leg. Two other sailors tripped over him. She had no time to regret her error. Instead she decided that legs were appropriate targets. Their wounds would not be permanent, and they would disrupt the sailors' efforts. One by one she flung her knives among the sand brigade.

"Marines, present your arms."

The line of crimson soldiers leveled their muskets at the ghost. She rained her final daggers into their midst. Men dropped or staggered backward, blood oozing through their breeches. The weapons discharged, but their bullets passed overhead.

"Regroup," said the sergeant. "Form your line."

She dug another pair of oil flasks from a pocket and pitched them on the deck. Fire flared into the rigging. The mob drew back.

"By my faith," someone yelled from the trunk of the main mast. "The ship's adrift."

Dazed crewmen glanced about. The Boston skyline was speeding past them, and Dorchester Heights loomed large on the starboard side.

"She's slipped her cables. We'll run aground."

"Deck there! Rig the storm anchors. Bosun, pipe the boats over on the double."

Whistles trilled and men stampeded in all directions. Longboats were uncovered and wrestled to the rails.

"Release storm anchors."

Horned iron shafts plummeted into the water and disappeared.

"Sir, the cables have been cut."

"What?"

"We've lost two storm anchors. If we drop the other two, we'll lose them."

"Recable, recable!"

Whips and flagrums cracked.

"Mind you the ghost," Dudley shouted. "Don't let her escape."

"Hang the ghost. We've got to save the ship."

Dudley grabbed a fallen musket and took aim. Rachel's only remaining weapon was her letter opener. She drew it from a pocket and slung it at him. The blade pinned Dudley's hat to the main mast. He staggered backward, his musket erupting with a fiery blast.

The ship shuddered and lurched to starboard. Timbers groaned. Ice aloft crackled and split, tumbling from the rigging to the deck. Crewmen were pitched off their feet.

"The ship's aground."

"This way," Rachel said to the boys. "Over the side with you."

She climbed atop the rail and leapt overboard. With a great splash she plunged into a rolling swell. Thousands of needles stung her body as the frigid seas engulfed her. Her lungs exploded in a shriek of pain, but her scream was swallowed in the icy waters. She thudded against the bottom and battled her way to the surface. Ice floes bludgeoned her body. She was thumping the fringe of a frozen sheet that encrusted the shore. The boys were hurling themselves into the sea about her.

"To shore, to shore," she said, pulling herself onto the ice. The frozen surface collapsed and dumped her back into the water. She clawed the ice, breaking chunk after chunk from the frozen plain, cutting a path to the distant shore. At last she managed to pull herself from the water.

"Peter," she said. "Peter Slater."

"I'm here," he said, flailing in the water. The other boys followed him toward her. She extended a hand and caught Peter's wrist. He passed the cabin boy to her, and she pulled him onto the ice.

"Wait for us by the shore yonder," she told the lad. "Don't stay on the ice. And take courage. You are free now."

He scampered off. Peter was next, and together he and Rachel pulled the remaining boys from the water.

"Pembroke," she told Peter through chattering teeth. "Do you know the place?"

"Aye," he said, his voice trembling. "It is far."

"You must get there. I am sorry, but I cannot go with you. See to the safety of the others."

"We shall make it."

"I know you will."

"Look," came a shout from the ship. "There she is. Boats away. Fetch her back here."

Go," she said. "And Godspeed to you all."

"God bless you, Regina Silsby," Peter said. "Come on, lads, on your feet. I know old Pembroke. There's fire and a hot meal awaiting us. We've not a moment to lose."

The boys scrambled to the highway.

"Run," Peter said. " 'Twill keep us warm. Courage, men. We're free, thanks to that sainted spirit."

Rachel watched as Peter scooped the cabin boy into his arms and carried him away.

"What a tale you'll have to tell your grandchildren," he said to the lad. "Chin up, men. We'll have fat bellies and warm beds before you know it. Come on, lads."

They were quickly gone, and Rachel turned back toward the *Devonshire*. The fire was out, and the ship lay reeling on the fringe of the ice floe, its masts leaning at a drunken angle. A longboat crowded with marines was dipping into the water.

"Cast off," said an officer in the boat's stern. "Ready oars."

The boat bounced toward her, following the path that she had cut through the ice. Its bow wave glowed a luminous white against the black bay waters. Bayonets stretched like porcupine quills from the mass of marines crowding the boat. She forced her frozen limbs to move, and under the weight of her soaked clothing she lumbered to the highway. Home and safety were far, far away.

Twelve

❧

The Phantom Ferryman

Rachel plowed through the snow smothering Dorchester Flats. Her garments were saturated with seawater and clung to her like leaden chains. In the frigid wind they were stiffening into stone. Her teeth chattered uncontrollably. Great spasms shuddered through her bowels and limbs. With every plunging step her boots squeezed water into the deepening snow, and their soggy leather gathered layer upon layer of icy crystals. Frost caked her skirts and gloves. The mask had fused to her face, and removing it would tear the skin from her skull.

Sleet and ice tumbled earthward. The highways, the hills, and even the heavens blended together into an eternity of swirling white. Somewhere in the vast expanse lay the road to Boston Neck. But all landmarks were lost in the blizzard.

From the maelstrom at her back came a grinding of timber on rock. Steel rattled and boots crunched in the snow. The *Devonshire's* marines were scrambling ashore.

"Stow those oars. Form up on the road."

"Look, sir, here's footprints."

"Aye, right enough. Ho, lads. I've yet to see a ghost that leaves tracks in the snow. Come along, quick march. She'll not get far in this tempest."

"Shore party, hold fast. Hold fast, I say."

The last voice was Capt. Dudley's. Another longboat scraped the shore.

"Lieutenant," Dudley said, "I am taking charge of this expedition."

"But my lord, these marines are assigned to the *Devonshire*. Our orders must come from Capt. Madden."

"Col. Leslie has delegated Regina Silsby's capture to me," Dudley said. "I'll not share the task with anyone. You and your men shall assist me."

"May I remind your lordship that Col. Leslie commands the 64th Regiment of Foot. His authority does not extend to the Royal Navy."

"As acting governor of Massachusetts," Dudley said, "Col. Leslie's order must supersede Capt. Madden's in this matter."

"My lord, I must protest."

"You'll do as I say, Lieutenant."

"Without Capt. Madden's approval I cannot. If it please your lordship, I shall send a boat back to the *Devonshire*."

"While Regina Silsby escapes? Hang you for your insolence. Now hold your tongue and fall in behind me. We've a ghost to capture, and I'll not waste another minute arguing protocol with such peasants as you. Sergeant, order the men forward."

A wolf howled. Rachel plunged deeper into the blizzard, quaking from boots to brow. The chill penetrated the very core of her being, slowing every pulse and freezing every fiber. Her legs grew stiff and heavy. Each step became more clumsy. Cold air knifed her lungs with every breath. Her vision blurred, and stars began to orbit her head.

Her boot slipped. She careened down a shallow slope, snow cascading about her. In a drift she thudded to a stop. Thick snow swaddled her, and evergreen boughs formed a black canopy overhead. The newly formed cradle was strangely warm and silent. She wanted to remain there, lying on her bed of velvet crystal, resting her tortured body. A few minutes' rest would strengthen her for the journey ahead. She closed her eyes.

"My lord," said a voice, "her trail has strayed from the road."

"Which way?"

"Toward the forest, my lord."

Clattering metal and musketry jarred her awake. The marines were drawing near—too near. She urged her body into motion and was immediately stung by searing pain. With a cry she went limp. The agony abated. Again she struggled to move. Reluctantly her limbs complied, and she managed to roll onto her stomach. Despite the pain she crawled back to the highway, and with a mighty heave, vaulted herself upright. Her heart revived, and blood coursed through her veins. The stinging subsided. With a feeble hand she wiped away the ice crusting her mask's eyeholes. A trail of her own prints stretched before her. She turned about and saw only frigid emptiness. Into the abyss she trudged, away from the marks in the snow.

A dark hole loomed in the blizzard before her. She blinked but could not flush the crag from her eyesight. Like a gash in an endless, empty canvas the rupture flapped open and closed. Had a void split the tempest? She plodded toward it, and the apparition slowly took the form of a man.

Startled, she halted. Was she blundering back toward her pursuers? No, this stranger was not garbed in crimson. Black robes billowed about his frame, and a thick hood concealed his features. He seemed to float among the ice floes at the water's edge, leaning on a long staff. From his cloak emerged a gaunt hand, and its gnarled fingers beckoned her.

She cringed. Unless she was mistaken, the apparition was a genuine ghost. With her eyes clamped shut she willed the demon away. The phantom remained, standing on the choppy water, his cloak tossing in the gale, his outstretched hand urging her to his side. She stumbled past him on the far fringe of the road. After a short distance she peered over her shoulder. The apparition had vanished.

Fully alert, her discomfort forgotten, she searched the surrounding storm. Who but a ghost could appear and evaporate so quickly? And why had the spirit summoned her? Was death at hand? The possibility made her shudder. Why was the heavenly messenger so dark and foreboding? Death for the Christian was supposed to be a dazzling portal into eternal life. Only for the lost was it a threshold of doom. She plodded onward, trembling and praying for deliverance.

Again the phantom appeared ahead of her, floating on the ice floes as before. His bony hand clawed at her. She dodged him and stole a backward glance to be certain he was not following. Lanterns brightened the blizzard behind her.

"My lord, she's slowing," said a voice. "Her footsteps have left the roadway again."

"She's making toward the trees."

"Wait, there's her trail climbing back to the road."

"She must have fallen into this ditch. Come on, lads, another minute or two and we'll have her."

Rachel could not lift her feet. Her clothes were heavy as iron, brittle as porcelain. She had become a pillar of ice supported by quaking limbs of jelly. Soon the ordeal would be done. The marines would overtake her, shackle her wrists and ankles, and carry her back to the ship. And there she would die.

She was too weary to be frightened. Sleep was what she needed, a long, restful sleep—an eternity of sleep—in a cozy bed beside a glowing fire. The thought filled her with a strange warmth. Heat tingled her toes and slowly radiated through her legs. For a moment the ground teetered and spun, then cascaded upward in a rush of tumbling white. Darkness swallowed her, and her ears resonated with a hiss of falling snow. Slowly her numbed brain realized that she had toppled forward and lay prostrate in the road. The powdery mattress reminded her of her own bed, with its crisp sheets and downy softness. She let herself doze.

Hardly did she sense the hands that gripped her, the arms that lifted her from the roadway. Numbing heat—that wonderful, warm sensation—was all she knew. It surrounded her, penetrated her, permeated her. Far from the frigid misery it carried her, to a distant refuge that swayed like a hammock in a summer sun. She basked in the warmth, floated in it, immersed herself in it. Heat soaked her skin and soothed her soul.

To her consternation, the sun grew hot. Her feet were
toasting. No longer did the gentle swaying lull her to sleep.
It churned her stomach. Something hard and uneven pressed
against her back. Her head throbbed, and her limbs ached.
Her face was chafed and sore. Disgruntled, she opened her
eyes. Through the holes of her mask she saw the phantom
standing above her, waving his long staff over her legs. Water sloshed against a wooden shell surrounding her. Odors
of seaweed, tar and hemp assaulted her nostrils. She was
lying in a boat and wrapped in a coarse, itchy blanket. The
phantom stood at the stern post, guiding the vessel through
choppy waters with a long, single oar.

So this was death, she thought. At least the chill was
gone. But her journey to the nether world was not as she had
hoped. Where was paradise, with its luminous clouds and riv-
ers of crystal? Where was her heavenly Father and His host
of angels? Too much like a Grecian myth was this gloomy
river Styx and this foreboding ferryman. What sort of under-
world lay beyond? Not the New Jerusalem, she realized. She
had been cast out, forsaken. Heaven was not to be her home.
But whatever destiny awaited her could not be worse than
the agony she had just escaped.

Bony fingers prodded her awake. The phantom was
leaning over her, his face lost in the folds of his black hood.
Afraid and uncertain, she pretended to sleep. Shriveled arms
squirmed beneath her, and slowly she was raised from the
boat. The ghoul's emaciated ribs pressed her side. He was
little more than a skeleton inside his hollow cloak. Along a
corridor of gray stone he bore her, up a granite staircase and
through a grotto of echoing sighs.

Through half-opened eyes she watched a maze of dungeon passageways drift by. Feeble lanterns brightened some
walls. After many twists and turns the phantom stopped. She

clamped shut her eyes. Her feet were plopped on a pavement of uneven cobblestone, and the gaunt arms released her.
Alone she stood, heart pounding, bowels quaking.

A rooster crowed.

"Six o'clock, and all's well," said a distant watchman.

She blinked. There stood her own house, its tall chimney
streaming smoke. Dawn was brightening the distant sky.

"How on earth?" she wondered. Dogs barked and horses
clopped. A wagon was trundling toward her. The driver's
whip snapped.

"Git up there, Bessie."

It was Mr. Rumstead, the tallow merchant.

She was alive! Across the cobbles she floundered to the
back gate of her father's garden. Fumbling with the bolt,
she pushed past the lattice and loped across the stable yard,
yanking off her leather mask as she approached the kitchen
steps. The back door to the house was unlatched. Inside,
remnants of a fire still warmed the kitchen hearth. An iron
pot filled with beef stew simmered over the orange embers.

She grabbed a ladle and scooped a steamy draft to her
lips. Broth ran hot and thick down her throat. She gulped another mouthful, heedless of the excess liquid oozing over her
cheeks. Warmth began to spread through her bowels.

Slumped across the kitchen table was Grandfather, snoring loudly. His face lay in a supper dish half-filled with beef,
and his fingers still gripped his empty mug. An uncorked jug
stood nearby. She seized the jug and spilled clear liquid into
a tin cup. It was rum, and it burned as it coated her innards.
She wiped her mouth on a soggy sleeve and slurped more
stew from the ladle. The chunks of beef and potato tasted
more delicious than a Christmas goose.

"Goodness," she said, staring at the floor. Seawater was pooling on the bricks beneath her feet. She cast off her damp cloak and winced at a sharp sting in her left shoulder. Unlacing the neck of her blouse, she pulled back the fabric and discovered a broad scrape scarring her skin. How she had gotten the wound she did not know—perhaps when she dove from the ship, or as she battled the ice floes encrusting Dorchester Flats. Until that moment the wound had not pained her at all, but suddenly it began to throb. It needed to be cleaned and dressed.

Grandfather snorted and began to stir. Rachel grabbed her cloak and started for the stairs, but she stopped at the kitchen doorway. Where could she go? Certainly not to her room, soaking wet as she was. And how would she hide her soggy garments? Her mother would ask questions, too many questions. Capt. Dudley, too, would be suspicious if he returned to the house and found her sopping wet and smelling of seaweed.

"Oh, Lord," she said, "what am I to do?"

Her eyes fell on the laundry basket. Of course!

She scooped up the soiled clothes and retreated to the stable yard. With luck, she could wash her garments with the other laundry, before anyone was wiser. If her mother should express surprise at her early rising, or at doing wash two days in a row, Rachel could feign that she had been unable to sleep and wanted something useful to do.

As the kitchen door banged shut, her grandfather jerked awake and glanced about.

"Who's there?" he said.

Seeing no one, he shook his head and picked bits of beef from his hair. His brow furrowed as he spied the pool of water staining the brick floor.

Thirteen

The Washing

In the chilly silence of the barn Rachel stirred a staff through the laundry cauldron. She had slipped her wet clothing in with the rest of the wash and stood in her soggy undergarments, a horse blanket wrapped about her shoulders, sniffing the mint-scented steam that wafted from the tub. An hour or more would pass before the clothes were ready to wring out, and she was already shivering with cold. A bone-jarring cough rattled her lungs and scraped her throat. It was the fourth such eruption to shake her in as many minutes. Similar coughs she had witnessed at many a sickbed, and she knew they signaled the onset of pneumonia. Unless she could warm her being, the malady would kill her.

Again she sought refuge near the flames beneath the cauldron but found them too feeble. She had squatted before them, lain beside them, almost sat atop them, but could not satisfy her body's craving for heat. Unless she shed her damp clothes and surrounded herself with penetrating warmth, she would succumb to the deadly illness.

Steam rose from the cauldron. Her clothes were faring better than she! While they swam in scented heat, she stood beside them freezing to death. She dipped her fingers in the water and let the fluid's warmth tingle through her wrist. Deeper into the bath she reached, until her arm was immersed to the elbow. Glorious warmth soaked through her skin, even seeping toward her shoulder. If only she could plunge her entire body into such encompassing heat.

An audacious thought struck her. It flew in the face of propriety and violated every remedy taught by family or physician. But it made perfect sense: she needed heat; the water was hot.

She placed a bucket upside down beside the cauldron. Standing on top of the pail, she shed the horse blanket and gripped the brim of the cauldron with both hands. Slowly she raised one leg and eased it into the steamy liquid. Warmth engulfed her to the hip. She slid her other leg into the water and gently let herself sink to her chin.

With a groan she rested her head on the lip of the cauldron. Scents of mint and lilac penetrated her sinuses, evaporating the fluid that blocked her nose and throat. The walls of her skull began to thaw. She breathed deeply the penetrating mist and savored its wafting sensation inside her lungs. Slowly her eyes closed, and she drifted dreamily into clouds of swirling bubbles.

Time passed. The water grew too hot to bear. She realized she was slowly cooking herself but wanted to linger longer in her bath.

"There's plenty of snow outside," she said to herself. Quickly she climbed from the cauldron, grabbed the bucket and scooted outside in her bare feet. Steam seeped from her pink skin and soggy undergarments as she scooped fresh snow from the barnyard. Puzzled neighbors watched. Embarrassed, she flashed them a timid smile and trotted back to the barn. After dumping the snow into the wash, she eased herself once more into the scented liquid. It felt wonderful. She loosened the knot of hair behind her head and let her dark locks swirl through the stream. Her head tilted slowly back until only her face was showing above the surface. Warmth sank into her scalp.

How long she lingered in the bath, with her limbs drifting and her hair swimming, she did not know. It seemed an eternity, and yet it passed in mere moments. Strange noises eventually interrupted her solitude, like muffled voices far away. She opened her eyes and saw Abigail Sutton's face hovering over her.

"Rachel Winslow," Abigail was shouting. "What in heaven's name are you about?"

Rachel splashed upright, her soggy hair streaming down her shoulders.

"Are you out of your mind?" Abigail said.

"Certainly not," Rachel said. "I have made a marvelous discovery."

"You are soaking wet. You'll catch your death."

"No, Abigail, it is wonderful."

"You're bewitched. I shall call for your mother at once. You need a doctor . . . or a minister."

"We wash our clothes thus, do we not?" Rachel said. "I was cold and dirty. It seemed a logical thing to do."

"But you are practically naked. Where is your dress?"

"In here, with me."

"If someone should happen upon you . . ."

"Who besides you would come barging into my father's barn?"

"Mr. Sinquin, for one," Abigail said. "He is in the house now, talking to your father."

"Josiah Sinquin?"

Rachel had forgotten his promise to call.

"And you've a host of soldiers under your roof," Abigail said. "I shouldn't be surprised if one of them wandered in here."

"Abigail, be a dear and find me something from the house to dry myself. And bring my green dress with you."

"I'll not be a party to this. You'll make a devil's consort of me."

"I've done no worse than those boys who swim off the end of Long Wharf in summer."

" 'Tis wicked, what you're doing, Rachel, taking off your clothes and getting yourself deliberately wet. You will catch your death of cold."

"In a pot full of steaming water?"

"When you get out of it, then."

"You once got yourself wet, when you fell off the foot-bridge at Ganders' farm."

"That was an accident."

"You were just as wet as I am now. We carried you to the house and stripped everything off of you, and you didn't die."

"It is not the same thing," Abigail said. "Drowning in a stream is not at all like stewing in that witch's brew."

" 'Tis nothing but water," Rachel said, "soaped and scented. Besides, if falling accidentally into a pool doesn't kill you, surely a hot bath taken deliberately will not. And heaven knows I needed it, after last night."

"What happened last night?"

"I . . . that is to say, my window burst open. Aye, while I was asleep. Snow was flying all about my room. I took such a chill I thought I might die of pneumonia. So I decided to warm myself in the wash. I've been here since dawn."

"Do you mean to say," Abigail said, "that you've been all morning . . . *in there?*"

"What's the time?"

"Half past ten."

"Really? No wonder I feel so well. I am warmer than the tropics."

"Gracious, Rachel, then you've not heard the news."

"What news?"

"Of Regina Silsby. She made a spectacle at the Customs House last night and in the harbor."

"Has someone seen her?"

"Seen her? There's nothing like it since . . . well, since Regina Silsby last showed her face. All Boston is jabbering about it."

"Tell me."

"She was two places at once. She cut the *Devonshire's* anchor cables, and the ship has piled up on Dorchester Flats. The crew is lifting off the guns and stores now, hoping to float her back into the harbor."

"Astounding," Rachel said. Her brow furrowed as she puzzled over the tidings.

"What's wrong?" Abigail said.

"Are you quite certain the cables were cut?"

"Clean through," Abigail said. "Father saw them this morning, dangling like dead snakes from the hawsers. Sailors and officers were standing about scratching their heads at the sight. Some of the crew have disappeared as well—Regina Silsby carried them all off. And the Customs House! That poor man trussed up in the pillory has completely vanished. People are saying Regina Silsby stole him away to her grave. There's talk of digging her up and finding his body in the coffin with her. But no one is willing to do it. Oh, Rachel, it makes me shudder."

Rachel was not listening. The *Devonshire's* anchor cables were thicker than a man's wrist, and tarred as well. Even if one of them managed to fray or rot apart, would all of them do so? Hardly. Nor would the crew ever let them decay to such a state. How, then, had they been severed? By a traitorous sailor or one of the kidnapped boys? All the boys had been imprisoned and frightened as foals. Sons of Liberty? The rebels were not so bold as that, and she had seen no one else bobbing about the bay that night. Except . . .

Her thoughts turned to the stranger in the skiff. Until that moment she had convinced herself that she had imagined him. But he must have been real. Only he could have cut those anchor cables. And after doing so, he had followed her across Dorchester Flats and carried her back to her own house. The stranger knew who she was. And if he knew her, he could betray her. But who was he? Who was shadowing her while she roamed about Boston as Regina Silsby?

"What is troubling you?" Abigail said.

"Oh," Rachel said. "Nothing at all. 'Tis an incredible story you're telling me."

"She's a demon," Abigail said, "straight from hell. Goodness, you don't suppose she has heard me say that."

"I am certain you've nothing to fear from Regina Silsby."

"But she lived in your house, Rachel. She must have come into this very barn, doing the wash as you're doing now — well, not quite as you're doing now, but she must have come here. Perhaps she still haunts this place."

"I have never seen her."

"Even so, she may be here, listening to every word we utter."

"I suppose that is a possibility."

"God bless the memory of Regina Silsby," Abigail said. "God bless and keep her, I say."

She gathered her shawl to her chin and said, "I do not like this place. I am going back to the house, before that demon ghost bewitches me."

"Regina Silsby shall not bewitch you."

"No?" Abigail said. "See what she's done to you. I don't wonder you're possessed of an evil spirit."

"Wait," Rachel said as Abigail retreated to the door. "Don't leave me like this. Abigail, do wait. I need something to dry myself. Abigail! Oh, bother."

She climbed dripping from the wash. How exasperating, to be hobbled by timid friends. She wrung out the garments and hung them to dry, choosing a dark corner of the loft for Regina Silsby's cloak. After dousing the fire and dumping the water, she wrapped herself in the horse blanket and scurried across the snow to the house, braving the neighbors' stares.

Safely inside the kitchen, she crept to the hallway, listening. Abigail had rejoined the women in the parlor. That would leave the study for Rachel's father to receive Josiah Sinquin. Complicating matters was Capt. Dudley, who might appear at the front door at any moment, unless he was already ensconced in her father's chamber. She would have to make a dash for her room and hope no one saw her.

"Lost your shirt, have you?" Grandfather said. She spun about. The old man was rising from behind the kitchen table, a dustpan and brush in his hands.

"Grandfather," she said. "How you startled me. I didn't see you."

"So I gathered," he said, dumping his sweepings into the fireplace. "What on earth are you doing?"

"I need a dress," she said. "I was doing the wash, and . . ."

". . . fell in?"

"Something of the sort."

"As it happens," he said, "your mother was mending one of your skirts when the Suttons arrived. It is hanging in the larder."

"Hallelujah," she said, and scurried into the store room. She slipped out of her wet undergarments and toweled herself dry with the blanket. A fresh blouse and pantaloons were hanging in the larder as well. While donning the clothing, she noticed the lingering effects of her bath. Her skin was pink and soft, smelling sweetly of mint and lilac, and feeling more smooth than ever she remembered it. Indescribable warmth permeated her being. Any hint of pneumonia had been utterly vanquished. She felt rejuvenated, invigorated, yet at the same time relaxed and calm. Contentment soothed her heart and soul. She was clean, fresh, new. Without doubt her bath had been excellent medicine, and she decided to bathe more often, regardless of what others thought or said.

Properly dressed, she emerged from the larder and sat by the fire to brush her hair. Grandfather was pouring boiled water into a pot of sassafras tea for Abigail, who stood ready with a tray to carry it to the parlor.

"Feeling better?" Grandfather said to Rachel.

"Much," she said, squeezing the water from her tresses.

"I fixed a hot toddy for you," he said, indicating a pitcher on the table.

"May I have a toddy as well?" Abigail said. "This sassafras stuff is horrid."

"Help yourself."

Abigail set down the tray and poured two steaming mugs from the pitcher. Grandfather eased onto a stool and watched Rachel drag her brush through her dark locks.

"My sister took baths," he said. "Used to sit right where you're sitting now, brushing her hair just as you're doing."

"Are you upset with me?" Rachel said.

"Why should I be?"

"Shocked, then?"

"Not at all. As I said, my sister took baths—swore by them, she did."

"Was she as strange as everyone says?" Abigail said.

"What is everyone saying?"

"That she's a witch. That she won't rest until she's taken a husband to the grave with her."

Grandfather pressed tobacco into his pipe and lit it from the candlestick on the table. He leaned back on his stool and watched the smoke curl from his lips to the rafters.

"Regina Silsby's better left alone," he said.

"Then she *was* a witch," Abigail said.

"I didn't say that."

"But you don't deny it. How dreadful, to dwell in the same house as that foul creature. Oh — I do beg your pardon, sir. She was your sister, after all. My father says there's a fellow mad with fear at the Customs House, yelling that Regina Silsby attacked him. Father saw the broken window she fled through. Do you suppose that poor fellow she took from the stocks will satisfy her?"

"Probably not," Grandfather said.

"What, then, is she after?"

"I think," he said, "she's after nothing at all."

"Abigail," Mrs. Winslow said. "Have you forgotten our tea?"

"Mercy," she said, jumping up. After a quick curtsy she grabbed the tray and scurried from the kitchen. Grandfather continued to puff his pipe.

"What did you mean, Grandfather," Rachel said, "when you said Regina Silsby was after nothing at all?"

"Spirits do not steal horses," he said.

"Horses?"

"The other night at Boston Neck," he said, "one of them redcoat steeds was taken."

"Didn't they find it again?"

"Aye, they found it," he said, "in the King's Chapel cemetery, nibbling the grass at Regina Silsby's grave. But why steal a horse to fly home? Shouldn't she prefer to fly there herself? And that business at the Customs House last night. What need has a ghost of breaking windows? Can she not simply drift through the wall?"

Blue smoke curled about his brow.

"Hain't Regina Silsby haunting Boston," he said. "Some devilishly clever fellow is playing them all for fools."

"Grandfather, do you mean to say that Regina Silsby is a man?"

"And a right crafty one at that."

"Perhaps he is a Son of Liberty," she said. "They're always running about dressed as red Indians."

"Aye, but no Son of Liberty ever ran aground one of his majesty's ships a'fore or stole away ten of the crew."

"They weren't crewmen, they were—"

She stopped herself.

"How's that?" he said.

"Old Mr. Gray," she said quickly, "he was not a crewman. He was put in the stocks for striking Capt. Dudley."

"'Hain't Gray I'm speaking of," he said. "The news is there's ten crewmen taken from that ship, and 'twas Regina Silsby that spirited them away. Seems to me the king of England won't be taking kindly to one of his warships being run aground, nor to having his hired help whisked away from under his very nose."

"Hired help? Those boys were kidnapped from their homes like slaves and—"

"Hush, child. That won't be how the king sees it, nor any of his noblemen."

"They've no right to beat innocent boys and imprison old men."

"They've a right to do anything they please," he said. "They're noblemen, we're commoners. They speak, we obey, and that's how things are."

"But . . ."

"Listen to me, lass. Yesterday those boys' lives took a turn for the worse. Today they're condemned men. If they're caught, they'll be hanged for desertion."

"Even the child?"

"Him, too. And that Gray's life is forfeit as well. Every one of them would be better off if Regina Silsby had left them alone. But it's done now and can't be undone. Mark me well, this Regina Silsby had best be careful, or he'll get himself hanged with the rest of them. 'Twould be better if he never showed his face again."

She sat stone-faced.

"Something troubling you?" he said.

"Excuse me," she said, rising from her chair. She wrapped her mother's shawl around her shoulders and tied a bonnet over her wet hair.

"Are you going out?" he said.

"I must finish the wash," she said.

Fourteen

King's Chapel

Rachel knelt in the back pew of the King's Chapel.

"Forgive me, Lord," she said. "I have sinned greatly."

Defying the king's soldiers, freeing Mr. Gray from the pillory, aiding the desertion of the boys—she had doomed them all to death.

"I am at fault," she said, "not they. But because of my sin, they will suffer. Oh, God, my guilt is greater than I can bear."

She lowered her head in shame. But warring with her conscience was a conviction that the soldiers had been wrong—wrong to rob the boys of their liberty; wrong to condemn Mr. Gray to certain death in the pillory. They were wrong to invade people's homes, devour their stores, and confiscate their wealth and goods. Protection of the people was their excuse to justify their thievery, but protection from what? And who would protect the people from roving ranks of armed soldiers, who took what they wished and beat anyone who complained?

"It is wrong," she said, pounding a fist on the pew. But was it right to respond with another wrong? *"Be not overcome of evil,"* the Scripture said, *"but overcome evil with good."*

"How is that done?" she said. "Please tell me."

Children gathered with their mothers at the altar rail. Together they admired the mistletoe and hemlock that still hung thickly throughout the church. The children squealed their delight as they ran from cluster to cluster, smelling the heady scents and crying out to their mothers how beautiful were the bundled boughs. *Congregationalists*, Rachel thought. They never decorated their own sanctuaries, but freely admired the decorations of others. So happy the children seemed, so safe in the pasture of their mothers' care, so unaware that their sovereign might one day claim his lordship over them, and snatch them from their families to a life of servitude, enslavement, and death. The shadow of his hand hung heavy over every man, woman, and child within his realm. One and all he owned them, to nurture or destroy as whim carried him.

A clatter in the organ loft arrested her thoughts.

"No, Thaddeus," said a man's voice. "Turn it this way."

She left her pew and approached the staircase leading to the loft. Morning sun streamed through the windows, brightening a thick column of ice that had formed beneath a crack in the ceiling. The frozen waterfall cascaded down the wall and spilled over the stairs in frigid, petrified flows. Carefully she gripped the handrail and eased up the icy stairwell.

The loft was crowded by a great copper kettle. Beneath it squatted a rotund, bald man feverishly tinkering with a contraption of brass and iron. His face was bright red and beaded with sweat.

"Mr. Newcomb," she said.

"Ah, Rachel," the little man said, peering at her over the rim of his spectacles. "You startled me."

"Whatever are you doing in the organ loft?" she said. " 'Twas less than a month ago you cleaned it."

"And I've been thinking about you and this organ since," he said. "Wait until you see this little device, my dear. Never again will you require the bell ringers to pump the organ bellows."

"You've turned the organ loft into a kitchen," she said.

"A kitchen, is it? Well, if my little kitchen works, we'll have the most triumphant Sabbath since . . . well, since the resurrection of Christ Himself—almost, at any rate. I don't fancy myself so much as that. Now watch closely. We'll stoke the fire. Thaddeus, bring more wood."

"Aye, father," the boy said. He scampered off and returned minutes later carrying an armload of fuel. Rachel wondered how he had managed to navigate the stairwell without killing himself. Newcomb stoked the brazier and fanned its flames into a blaze. Atop the fire sat the copper kettle, but it was hardly a proper one, for it was shaped like a drum, with two spouts opposite each other, both of them bent at a most unnatural angle.

"You won't be able to pour out from that," she said, "without spilling it all over."

"Did you know," Newcomb said, "that the ancient Greeks had harnessed steam?"

She shook her head.

"They understood the power of fire and water," he said. "And I have learned their ancient secrets."

"How?"

"Books, lass, books. There's a wealth of knowledge to be had from reading."

The brazier's fire shimmered in his spectacles, brightening his glee.

"Now, Rachel," he said, patting the copper kettle. "Ouch! Heavens, 'tis hot already. This kettle's about half-full with water. Tell me, if you can, what results when the fire sets the water to boiling?"

"You can make tea," she said, "or coffee, or use it to launder clothing or . . ."

"Confound it, lass," he said. "Steam, Rachel, steam! Boiling water makes steam. You've heard it whistle from the spout of a kettle, haven't you?"

"Aye."

"The steam from these spouts," he said, "will spin this drum around, driving the pistons that pump the organ's bellows."

She blinked her confusion.

"Come, child," he said, "just wait and you'll see."

"But the Rev. Caner," she said, "when he discovers this mess in the organ loft."

"Mess? This is science, lass, a wonder in the making."

"The reverend will be most upset."

"Well, there's no need to tell him about it just yet, is there? Let's keep this our little secret until Sunday."

"But . . ."

"Swear to me now," he said, "our secret."

"Very well," she said. "I swear."

"Good. Look, Rachel, there it goes."

Boiling water was banging against the cauldron's copper walls. Steam leaked from the angled pipes, weakly at first, then slowly strengthened into blasts. Newcomb greased the kettle's axles with lard, and the drum began to turn like a windmill. Hinged legs attached to the drum rocked up and down, pumping the bellows.

"Gracious, Mr. Newcomb," Rachel said. "Your machine is driving the bellows by itself."

"Hah," he said with a laugh. "I knew it would work. You see that, Thaddeus?"

The boy nodded, his eyes wide with wonder. Faster and faster the legs pummeled the organ bellows.

"It is magic," Rachel said.

"No, lass, it is science. Now tell me, did you ever see any of those bell ringers work like that? They'd be exhausted from running in place by now. Let's get you up to the organ and play us a piece. Remember, this kettle will be pumping the bellows for you."

She ascended the loft and perched herself before the tiered keyboards. At her back stretched the open air of the sanctuary, and above her towered the great pipes of silver, brass, and lead. She pulled open several stops and felt air rush into the organ's lungs. Her fingers depressed the keys, unleashing a chord that pummeled the sanctuary from pavement to rafters.

"Magnificent," Newcomb said as her chord died away. "A complete triumph."

"I have never heard it play so loudly," she said.

"And you see, Rachel? All that's required is a hot flame and a kettle half-full of water."

"Mr. Newcomb, you are a genius."

"Hardly that," he said. "A student of science is all. Now I've got to figure a way to feed water into the kettle so we don't have to stop it for refilling."

"I'm sure you'll think of something."

"Of course, lass. Which reminds me, I've a surprise for you. Thaddeus, bring me that satchel."

The boy tugged a canvas sack from among his father's tools. Newcomb fumbled through the pouch and pulled out a sheaf of papers.

"Ah," he said, "here it is."

He blew dust from the sheets and handed them to her.

"I'd be most grateful," he said, "if you'd play this tune for me."

"Mr. Newcomb," she said. "You are a composer of music as well."

"Not at all."

He pointed to the top of the first page. Beneath the title was a signature that made her mouth drop open: *Regina Silsby*.

"If I recall correctly," he said, "she was your grandfather's sister. That would make her your great-aunt."

"Where did you get this?" she said.

"My dear child, I used to pump the organ bellows for her while she played."

"Do you remember her?"

"As if I had seen her only yesterday. She was a grand lady."

"Please tell me about her."

"I loved her," he said, "as much as a ten-year-old boy can love a woman, at any rate. We all loved her."

"All?" she said.

"The bell ringers," he said. "We were nine in number, and every one of us falling over each other to be the one she chose to pump the organ. You never saw a more pious or dedicated group of boys than we, roaming about the church at all hours, polishing the bells, mending the pull cords, sweeping the stairs—any chore at all—just to be present when she arrived for her daily serenade. Oh, she was clever, Regina Silsby was. She could make this old organ sound like an entire chamber orchestra."

In mute fascination Rachel studied the music, hearing the tune in her head as she read the notes. Regina Silsby had condensed an entire concerto into a swift, single movement. Its rhythm was based on a minuet, but the tempo was far more sprightly and the chord progressions far more intricate. Scribbled into the margins were comments on stops, cadence, and voicing. The piece used the entire range of the organ— trumpets, reeds, woodwinds—with a vibrancy that made traditional compositions tame. Hers was not the work of a melancholy or tormented soul; rather, it was an exuberant cacophony spilling from a vivacious heart and spirit. All the joys of heaven seemed to have flooded from her in a single, mad gush.

"This is ingenious," Rachel said.

"Brilliant," Newcomb agreed.

The piece ended abruptly in the middle of a measure, and the final pages were blank.

"It is unfinished," she said.

"She was composing that one on the night she died," he said. "I was here with her."

"You?"

He nodded.

"I passed many evenings in this organ loft with her," he said. "She played quite frequently during her last days."

"Tell me how she died."

" 'Twas a dreadful November night," he said, "wind howling and snow blowing about as thick as a horse blanket. She arrived just as the sun was setting. But for the candles on the organ's music stand, the chapel was dark. There was a leak in the roof of the stairwell, and water had run down and frozen on the stairs, just as it is now—very dangerous. Regina Silsby had spent many weeks composing that piece in your hand. She was just about finished, as you can see there, when the chapel doors blew open. She ran down to close them, and slipped and fell on the stairs. It was dreadful to see her stretched out on the pavement like that. Her head was twisted at a terrible angle. I knew she'd broken her neck."

"How horrible."

"I made my way to her as quickly as I could," he said. "The stairs were most treacherous. She looked at me strangely, unable to move anything but her eyes. I took her hand, and it was completely limp. She asked me, 'Who are those shining men?' I looked about, but saw no one. 'Behind you,' she said, 'I see four shining men, all in white.' I thought she had lost her mind. I ran for the church sexton, but when I returned with him she was already dead. A crowd of people had gathered about her."

"They say she was a witch," Rachel said. "Even Grandfather seems to think so."

"No, child, I'm sure you're mistaken. Regina Silsby was a saint. There wasn't a more delightful woman in the world than she. Even the death of her betrothed couldn't diminish her spirit."

"She was to be married?"

"To a lad named Morgan Proctor. He was first mate on one of her father's ships. Your grandfather sailed with him, and many an adventure they had together. Have you heard any of your grandfather's tales?"

"Some," she said.

"He was a bold one, your grandfather, and Morgan Proctor was no less. They once beat off a pirate attack in the Caribbean. Any other sailor would have been glad to escape with his skin, but not these lads. They tracked the buccaneers back to their island fortress. In the dead of night they stole into the pirates' castle, freed a dungeon full of prisoners, spiked the fortress's guns, blew up the pirates' stores, and burned their ship. Not a man was lost in the adventure, and the entire crew was the toast of Boston for months upon their return. There wasn't a seaman in Boston who didn't wish to sail with them."

"You said that Morgan Proctor died."

"Aye," Newcomb said. "Their last journey together took them to the West Indies, and Morgan Proctor was swept overboard in a gale. Pity, too, for he was to wed Miss Regina on his return. 'Twas late summer when your grandfather brought the news to his sister here in the chapel. She was sitting on that very bench you're occupying now. Her brother's news put her to tears, and she fled home. Didn't come out for days."

"How awful."

"She mourned him," Newcomb said, "and had a memorial stone erected to him in the King's Chapel cemetery."

"I have seen it."

"He's not buried there, but she felt he deserved a Christian burial, because he was a good and godly man. Every day she would pray there, then come into the chapel and ask one of us to pump the organ bellows while she played. 'To chase away the melancholies,' she said. But she had a stout heart and a noble spirit. By autumn's end her sunlight had mostly returned. *"The Lord gave, and the Lord hath taken away,"* she would say of her lost bridegroom. *"Blessed be the name of the Lord."* Then she would lecture us about trusting God even in the worst of circumstances. *"The joy of the Lord is your strength,"* she would say.

"To pass the time," he said, "she worked at her compositions, while I and the other bell ringers pumped the organ bellows for her day and night. We must have run from here to Concord and back a dozen times with the hours we spent pumping for her. She loved the sound of this old beast."

"Why do so many people think her a witch?"

"Well," he said, coughing and scratching his head, "there's many who think a person as merry as she is out of sorts, especially when she's widowed before she's married. Extremely clever she was as well, and to dull folk that can be mystifying. And she had a generous humor. Loved to twist things around, she did, as you'll discover when you play that piece she's written. She explained it to me one evening while I was pumping for her. Even the happiest tune she could transform into a dirge by shifting key and rhythm. The change was wondrously bleak. Fit for a funeral she played, and all the while laughing like a child at the silliness of it. Scarcely could I keep the pumps working, in such a fit of mirth was I, and the organ whimpered to weakness. By changing key and measure again she could turn a requiem into a jig, then just as quickly change it into a minuet or a royal march. Many thought her disrespectful, playing non-sacred music in the house of God at all hours."

"That is ridiculous," Rachel said.

"To be sure. She believed all music was God-breathed. The chapel's vicar was her staunchest defender. He even trusted her with a key to the chapel and let her lock up when her playing was done. Sometimes she'd play long into the night. 'Twas then that the gossips would tell their tales and want not for embellishment with each telling. But I knew better."

"Because you were with her."

"I daresay Regina Silsby was more familiar to me than anyone those last weeks. A more beautiful and regal creature I never knew. Many years passed before I realized who were the shining men she spied that terrible night."

"But you saw no one."

"Indeed I did not," he said. "Still, they were present, as surely as you and I are present now."

"Who were they?"

"Angels, come to carry her home. She departed with them while I was off fetching the sexton. After her body was carried away I found these sheets on the organ's music stand. I gathered them up and took them home with me. They've not seen the sun but once or twice a year since. My hope was that one day I might give them to someone like you and hear them played again."

"Had she any more compositions?"

"Dozens and dozens," he said. "Hymns, fugues, fanfares, ballads of all kinds."

"Where are they?"

"Only heaven knows," he said. "Lost, I expect. This one's particularly marvelous. It is all that's left to us, and now I give it to you. I should be very grateful if you played it for me."

"I shall," she said, "and I shall treasure it all my life."

"God bless you, child. How like her you are."

"Am I?"

" 'Tis almost like seeing her again. Same hair, same coloring, same laugh, same spirit."

He brushed tears from his eyes. She smiled, pleased that he should see in her a glimmer of the glorious creature he described. Her fingers danced across the keys, following a measure on the score. Its melody echoed through the church.

"I shall learn it for you," she said. "And you shall hear it before a fortnight has passed."

Fifteen

❧

Arrest

Capt. Dudley sat scowling in the master's chair of the Winslow parlor. He poured more wine into his tankard mug and stared at the ruby liquid. Thrice Regina Silsby had humiliated him: at the Green Dragon, at Boston Neck, and again on Dorchester Flats. The cursed ghost was more than a nuisance, she was a threat to his very existence. Unless he captured her, he would be sent back to Britain in disgrace. Hang his father for banishing him to this forsaken wilderness. Why had the old miser insisted that his son distinguish himself in the Americas before coming into his inheritance? Why could the tyrant not leave him to frolic in the parlors and palaces of London? And Col. Leslie, that hog's ear, had hung Regina Silsby's capture about his neck like a millstone. Who was more hateful he knew not: his father or Leslie.

More mouthfuls of wine fueled Dudley's fury. Regina Silsby was the pit of his predicament. When he learned the ghost's identity he would skewer the scoundrel on a sword, then cut off his head and mount it on a pike. The body he would burn to cinders and scatter the ashes across the seas for the urchins to devour. Perhaps then, his rage might be abated.

He pulled a watch from his pocket and eyed its ivory face. Half-past eleven, almost time for dinner. But no, dash it all. On Thursdays the Winslow household was out until supper. The shipmaster spent the day in his counting house, while his wife visited her chatty friends. The daughter—what was her name? Rachel, aye—wandered about Boston like a dockyard wench. Only that silly grandfather remained at home, a useless bag of bones.

The front door swung open and closed, and Jeremiah Winslow appeared in the hallway.

"Good day, Captain," Winslow said. "I do believe I have forgotten something in my study."

Dudley growled a response. Winslow noticed the half-empty bottle on the side table.

"Has Col. Leslie made a gift of wine to you?" he said.

"No, you have," Dudley said. "I took it from your wine cellar. Needs more aging, I expect. Really, Winslow, a man of your stature should stock better provisions. The candied fruits are quite good. Have one."

Dudley slipped a letter opener from his pocket and stuck it into the jar of confections at his side. He offered the morsel to his host. Winslow paled.

"Where did you get that blade?" he said.

"This?" Dudley said. "She threw it at me."

"Who?"

"Regina Silsby. Pinned my hat to the *Devonshire's* mast. You can see it's got her initials on the hilt."

"Merciful heaven," Winslow said. He bolted from the room and rushed upstairs. Dudley popped the fruit into his mouth, then followed Winslow to the study. The shipmaster was digging through his desk, spilling the cubbyholes' contents onto the floor.

"What's got into you, man?" Dudley said.

"It's not here," Winslow said. "It's gone."

"What, for pity's sake?"

"My letter opener."

"What did it look like?"

Winslow stabbed a finger at the letter opener in Dudley's hand.

"That," he said.

"This is yours?" Dudley said. Winslow collapsed into a chair and dragged a hand across his brow.

"Aye," he said. "It belonged to my wife's aunt."

"What was her name?"

"Regina Silsby."

Dudley's eyebrows jumped.

"Do you mean to say," he said, "that Regina Silsby was related to you?"

"By marriage. She was sister to my father-in-law. I am almost ready to believe she has come back from the grave."

"This dirk belongs to you then."

"How did she get it?" Winslow said. "For years I have kept it locked in this desk."

"You're quite certain?"

"I am the only person who possesses a key."

"And this desk is never unlocked?"

"Only by myself."

"Then it is my duty, Mr. Jeremiah Winslow, to arrest you in the name of the king."

"What?"

"For assaulting a king's officer, for sedition and insurrection against the crown, for conspiracy to destroy a warship in His majesty's service, for aiding in the desertion of impressed seamen—"

"Surely, my lord, you don't think that I—"

"A king's officer has been attacked," Dudley said. "I hold the weapon in my hand, and you confess that it belongs to you."

"But I had nothing to do with these assaults."

"And you expect me to believe that your wife's dead aunt, Regina Silsby, did?"

"The letter opener was stolen from me, my lord."

"How? You admitted yourself that you keep the desk locked, and that you possess the only key. You are the only person capable of accessing this letter opener. Bradshaw! Bring a detail here at once. We've got our ghost."

Sixteen

❧

Interruptions

Rachel threw off her cape and bounded through the front hall to her mother's drawing room. Thursday was a perfect day to practice Regina Silsby's manuscript. The house was empty but for her grandfather who, when he wasn't napping, seemed deaf to everything. She plopped herself down at the clavichord and perched the score on the stand before her. Gazing from the wall above was the mirthful portrait of Regina Silsby, who somehow seemed pleased that her music would soon tickle a listener's ear. Rachel gazed at the painting, with its delicate hands cradling pen and manuscript.

Perhaps the painting displayed one of Regina Silsby's lost scores. If the artist had been careful enough to detail Regina Silsby's work, a portion of her music might be reconstructed.

Rachel rose from the stool and twisted her head to read the page on the canvas. Her eyes widened. She snatched the music sheet from the clavichord and held it against the picture. The manuscripts were identical. Painted into the portrait was the same score that Rachel now held in her hand.

She dropped back onto the bench, dazed. The canvas must have been painted within weeks, perhaps days, of Regina Silsby's death. How youthful she appeared, so spirited and lively, unaware that tragedy awaited her. What jest had curled her lips in that silent smile? Perhaps the answer lay in her music.

Rachel turned her attention to the song before her. It had been silent for over thirty years, and the moment of its resurrection seemed almost sacred. A prayer was scribbled beneath the manuscript's signature. She read it aloud.

"Give me grace, Lord, to honor You in what I do."

Timidly her fingers wandered across the keys, and Regina Silsby's final melody drifted through the room. The tune was as delightful as Rachel had expected, and its chord progressions were marvelous. Regina Silsby had threaded multiple dissonances together in a complex pattern that was simultaneously provocative and pleasing. Her resolutions were wonders of creativity, never lingering long enough to rest before springing off in another direction. The entire composition was sprinkled with syncopated rhythms that urged one's feet to tap along. Rachel could not help but smile as she progressed through the piece. It was a gleeful gallop through a chaotic but carefully mapped racecourse.

A second venture through the piece increased her confidence. While approaching the score's abrupt end she thought she recognized a pattern that might enable her to fabricate a conclusion. Her third and fourth passages were laced with interruptions as she paused to master the more difficult sections. Each venture through the music enabled her to increase her tempo toward the manuscript's designated pace, which was truly a mad dash.

"Wonderful," she grinned, "absolutely wonderful."

"Rachel," Grandfather said from a distant room. "Is that you?"

"Gracious," she said, scooping up the manuscript. In her exuberance she had forgotten to play softly and instead had been hammering away at the keyboard. She fled the parlor and bounded up the stairs to her room. Why she retreated so hastily she could not say. There was no shame in possessing the manuscript; indeed, she felt honored to have it. Even more, she wanted to defend the memory of her great aunt. But she feared her grandfather's reaction to the parchment. If he believed that his sister was a witch, he might demand that Rachel surrender the score, in which case he would probably burn it. Doubtless that had been the fate of Regina Silsby's other works. This one must remain. Rachel decided to hide the manuscript in her wardrobe, under the paper that lined the bottom shelf.

Grandfather wandered into the empty parlor. Had his ears deceived him? Surely the melody spilling into the kitchen had not been a figment of his imagination.

"Rachel," he said. No answer.

He scratched his head and studied the youthful portrait of his sister, who gazed back at him with her knowing smile. Deep in the grottos of his memory, other tunes began to echo, tunes unheard for decades, tunes silenced one dreadful November night, when a tumble down the chapel stairway had ended his sister's life. He recalled the day she had posed for the portrait, which was to have been his Christmas gift to her. How gleefully she had received the news of it, throwing her arms about his neck and kissing both his cheeks. In a chair by the window she had sat, her current manuscript in her lap and a quill pen in hand, as if she had paused from her work long enough for the artist to capture a brief moment of her life.

The front hall door burst open.

"Rachel," Mrs. Winslow said. "Come quickly. Something terrible has happened."

"Mother?" Rachel said from the head of the stairs.

"Your father has been arrested."

"What?"

"He is detained at the Customs House."

"But why?"

"They say he has been marauding about as Regina Silsby's ghost."

Rachel's jaw dropped.

"We must go to him immediately," Mrs. Winslow said. "Bring along some bread and beef from the kitchen."

"Aye, mother, at once."

Rachel hurried to the kitchen and soon emerged with a basket under an arm.

"Father cannot be the ghost," she said while donning her cloak. "It can be proved."

"I fear that Capt. Dudley is not interested in proofs," Mrs. Winslow said. "How on earth can he think your father such a villain?"

Rachel followed her mother outdoors, and from the parlor window Grandfather watched them vanish up the street.

"Regina Silsby's ghost, is he?" the old man said. "And I am the king of England."

He shuffled from the parlor to the front hall and up the stairs. Along the corridor he wandered, into his own room, where he closed and bolted the door. Beneath the window stood his sea chest. From a chain around his neck he removed an iron key and fit it into the trunk's padlock. The hasp popped open. He lifted the heavy lid and carefully removed the upper tray. It was crowded with scrimshawed knives, brass tools, a telescope, compass and sextant, delicate fans of paper and silk from China, and short-stemmed smoking pipes. Beneath the tray lay woolen scarves, canvas trousers and cotton shirts, a cutlass, three pistols, a bullet mold, a gaming board of ivory, a shaving kit, a mess kit, bundled letters from his parents, his sister, and his wife, a Bible, a book on navigation, a diary, and a logbook.

From the bottom of the box he retrieved the book which he had been searching. Its leather cover was brittle and cracked, its binding ribbons frayed with age. He loosened the ribbons and opened the cover. One by one he lifted out the loose papers within.

"Fugue in C major," read the first sheet, "Regina Silsby."

He scanned the stemmed notes dotting the page, hummed the tune, and set the sheet aside.

"Concerto for clavichord and stringed instruments," read the second manuscript, "Regina Silsby."

Only once had she ever managed to assemble musicians skilled enough to play it, and the result had been magnificent.

"Fanfare for my brother, on his twenty-fifth birthday," announced the third score, "Regina Silsby."

166

One by one he leafed through the papers, hearing each melody as he went. With his eyes closed he could see his sister playing her songs, by daylight, by candlelight, on holidays, on common days. He remembered her voice, her laughter, the gleam in her eyes. For a fleeting moment he was young again, dancing comical jigs for her amusement while she raced her fingers across the keys, daring him to go faster and wagering with him who would stumble first. Usually he lost. He remembered the prayers she prayed, the pranks she played, the feasts she made.

At last he uncovered the final page of his collection, and the music flooding his mind ceased. His sister receded into his memory, and the bare walls of his room enclosed him once more. He caressed the stack of papers with grizzled hands. From the mirror above the washbasin gazed a withered face once handsome and ruddy. Since the day he had last beheld his sister, many decades had worn away his youth. He had married, fathered a daughter, seen her marry and bear a daughter of her own. One day his granddaughter would marry and have children as well. Fast approaching, too, was his own departure, when his body would descend into the earth with his sister's, and his spirit would ascend on high, where she waited to greet him. And there he would wait to greet his daughter, and hers.

But for the moment, a single truth brightened his mortal being. The song wafting from the parlor just now was not among the pages in his sea chest.

"By heaven," he said with a laugh, "it is not lost, after all. She's found it, she has. Rachel's found it. Hallelujah!"

He danced a jig in the center of the room and clapped his hands with glee.

Seventeen

The Trap

Dudley sat in the Customs House office and propped his boots on the writing desk. Lt. Bradshaw stood by the window, inspecting the pane broken by Regina Silsby. From the hallway thumped a bailiff on a wooden leg. He handed an iron key ring to Dudley.

"The prisoner Jeremiah Winslow is secure, my lord," the bailiff said.

"Good," Dudley said. "See that he suffers as much as possible."

"My lord?"

"I want him in pain," Dudley said. "Cold, hunger—make him miserable."

"But there's no reason —"

"Do as I say, or you shall join him."

"Aye, my lord. Miserable he shall be."

The bailiff retreated from the room.

"Is that necessary, my lord?" Bradshaw said.

"Am I surrounded by imbeciles?" Dudley said. "Of course it is necessary."

"Surely your lordship doesn't believe this Winslow fellow is the ghost."

"Certainly not, fool," Dudley said. "But he will lead us to her."

"Begging your pardon, my lord?"

"Are you so witless? She will come for him."

Bradshaw swallowed and said, "Regina Silsby? Here?"

"Are you afraid of her too?"

"No, my lord, never. But . . . I don't understand."

"Bradshaw, you simpleton, have you not noticed a pattern to Regina Silsby's habits? No? Allow me to recite them for you. She first comes to the aid of the Sons of Liberty at the Green Dragon, enabling them to elude arrest. Next she appears at Boston Neck, where she thwarts our foray against the rebel stores at Pembroke farm. Lastly she frees a rebel prisoner from the public stocks and kidnaps men pressed into his majesty's service. Where there's a rebel in danger, we find Regina Silsby. She will come for this fellow as well, and the more miserable we make him, the sooner she shall come."

"To rescue him, I suppose."

"And we shall be waiting for her. By heaven, I'll see her neck in a noose."

"I'll double the guard, my lord."

"Triple it, and make certain each man's musket is loaded with powder and ball. I'll put a detachment of grenadiers at your disposal."

"Aye, my lord, thank you. But . . ."

"Speak up, man."

"Suppose she doesn't come?"

"She will come."

"But if she doesn't?"

"If we must hold him in chains for six months," Dudley said, "we shall do it."

"But, my lord, he has committed no crime."

"That is Regina Silsby's affair. If she wants to see justice done by this peasant Winslow, she shall either rescue him or surrender herself to me. And thus shall we rid ourselves of her."

"To detain an innocent man, my lord, will not go well with the citizens."

"Hang the citizens. Hang every man, woman, and child among them. If I have to jail every freeman in Boston I shall do it, do you hear? Mongrels and cheats they are, to the very last one."

"Even mongrels have teeth, my lord," Bradshaw said. "A dog beaten too often may turn on his master."

"A dog is still a dog," Dudley said. "If he doesn't like his master's beating, he shall accept his master's bullet. These American cowards slink about as red Indians and goblins, but not one of them will face me man for man. I swear by all that is sacred, if one more of these peasants crosses me, I shall put a musket ball through his brain."

"Perhaps if we were more temperate in our dealings with the Americans . . ."

"Roast your liver, Bradshaw. You sound like a rebel yourself."

Footsteps echoed on the marble floor of the rotunda. A feminine voice told the sentry, "I am Mrs. Jeremiah Winslow. I have come with my daughter to see my husband."

"There now, Bradshaw," Dudley said. "Already our couriers have arrived, to bear our message abroad."

"My lord?"

"Confound you, man. The prisoner is useless to us if nobody knows we have him. These ladies will carry our tidings through the streets. Eventually the news must reach Regina Silsby's ear."

Dudley rose from his chair and strolled into the hall.

"Why, bless my soul," he said. "Here is my charming hostess and her lovely daughter. How may I serve you, madame?"

"I wish to speak to my husband," Mrs. Winslow said. "I am told he is a prisoner here."

"Indeed," Dudley said. "Upon my word, Bradshaw, I cannot fathom how ladies so charming can be kin to such a rogue and scoundrel."

"You will kindly not insult my husband in my presence," Mrs. Winslow said. "It is my understanding that you hold him under false pretenses. I demand his release."

"My dear Mistress Winslow, your husband is charged with the high crime of treason against the crown. Even if I wished to, I could not release him to you."

"My husband is no traitor. It can be proved."

"I fear his case is a military matter, madame. A tribunal shall decide his fate."

"How can this be? My husband is not a soldier."

"He is a spy and a saboteur. On those grounds I can have him hanged."

Mrs. Winslow went white.

"You cannot mean that," she said, her voice trembling.

"I do mean it, madame. You should have chosen more wisely when you married."

She collapsed in a chair.

"If it please your lordship," Rachel said, "May we speak with my father?"

"As you wish," he said. "What is in that basket you're carrying?"

"Bread and meat."

"May I be permitted to see it?"

She extended the basket to him. Dudley removed the checkered cloth and scoured through the basket's contents. He took a chunk of beef and stuffed it into his mouth.

"Very good," he said with a nod. "Bradshaw, show these ladies to the prisoner. They may tarry five minutes."

"Aye, my lord."

The lieutenant led the women to the cellar. From a peg on the stone wall he removed a single lantern and escorted them through a forest of granite columns frosted with ice. Casks and crates cluttered the space.

"I shouldn't fret too much," he said, his words echoing through the cavern. "Your husband's offenses may not merit a hanging."

"My husband is innocent," Mrs. Winslow said.

"Even so, his lordship is most insistent in this matter, and he is confident of his proofs."

"Proofs," she said. "There are none."

"Then perhaps you've nothing to fear, madame. Ah, here we are."

He unbolted a stout door. Its hinges groaned as he tugged it open.

"Jeremiah," she said as she rushed into the store room.

"Sarah, dearest," he said, rising and wrapping his arms around her. "And my sweet Rachel too."

"Oh, darling," Mrs. Winslow said, "you're so cold. How can they keep you in this wretched place?"

"There, now, my dear," he said. "Mustn't fret. It isn't as bad as all that."

"They mean to hang you," she said.

"Do they? Well, don't expect anything to come of it. I've done no wrong, and it shall be proved. Their only evidence is a letter opener which was stolen from me."

"A letter opener?" Rachel said.

"The ghost hurled my letter opener at his lordship," Winslow said. "How she got it I shall never know."

"You will die of the cold and damp before your case ever comes to trial," Mrs. Winslow said.

"I've had a few hours to think," he said. "There's nothing happens without the Lord's consent. 'Twas from prison that Paul wrote most of his epistles. Without his chains, we'd have no New Testament. Who knows what greater good may come of this? We must wait and see."

"I've brought you meat and bread, Father," Rachel said, offering him the basket. She feared to say more.

"Thank you, my dear. Let us bless this bounteous feast together."

They bowed their heads.

"Gracious Lord God," Winslow said, "Your ways are always inscrutable. I'm sure you must bring some good of this, though I confess at present I cannot fathom what it is. May Your will be swiftly accomplished and Your purposes prevail. I thank you for the generosity of my wife and daughter, who have nourished me so richly these many years. Grant that we may soon enjoy each other's company once more, never to be parted again."

"Amen," the women said.

"Amen," Bradshaw said from the corridor.

Eighteen

Plans

"We must hire a lawyer at once," Mrs. Winslow said as she and Rachel shuffled along the street, "the best that Boston can offer. Mr. Otis, perhaps, or Mr. Adams."

"Mother, there's something I must tell you."

"Not now, child. Your grandfather will need his supper soon. Go home and tend to him. I shall be along soon enough."

"But Mother."

"Please, Rachel," Mrs. Winslow said, halting. The tremor in her voice and the tears in her eyes left Rachel silent.

"I shall be along directly," her mother said. "Pray, Rachel, pray very hard."

"Aye, Mother."

They parted at the corner. Rachel scurried home, her anxiety boiling into a torrent that crashed against the walls of her being. She burst into the house and cast her cloak on the floor. Fleeing upstairs to her room, she threw herself on her bed and buried her face in the linens. Her anguish erupted in a flood of tears.

"Oh, God, what have I done?" she said. Because of her offenses, her father sat in prison awaiting a gallows. Only by surrendering herself could she save him. And already she knew the outcome of her confession. Her father would refuse his release, even swear that he had committed her crimes, and take on himself her punishment. By her follies, she had murdered her own father.

Frantic thoughts of rescue spilled through her mind. Twenty soldiers she had counted in the vicinity of the Customs House. Under worse conditions she had escaped the *Devonshire*. But her success had been a stroke of fortune. It was the cutting of the anchor cable that had saved her, not her own cunning. And the soldiers at the Customs House had been inattentive on her previous visit. This time they would be alert. And there would be more of them.

"Lord, speak to me," she said. "I have been a fool."

Her Scriptures brought little solace. Psalm 91 declared:

"He that dwelleth in the secret place of the most High shall abide under the shadow of the Almighty. I will say of the Lord, he is my refuge and my fortress: my God, in him will I trust. Surely he shall deliver thee from the snare of the fowler, and from the noisome pestilence."

"Deliver my father," she said. "Be merciful. Please don't hide Your face from us."

How could she ask for deliverance, when her own sins had brought about the calamity?

"Send Your angel," she said, "as You did that night on Dorchester Flats. I know now 'twas Your angel that rescued me. I did not deserve it, but You delivered me. You spared my life. Please rescue my father. He has done nothing wrong."

A soft knock sounded on the door.

"Who is it?" she said, wiping her eyes.

"Grandfather. May I enter?"

"Aye," she said. The old man shuffled into the room and sat beside her.

"Fretting about your father?" he said.

"They mean to hang him," she said. "Oh, Grandfather, this is awful. It is all my fault."

"Rachel, dear, how is it your fault?"

"I have been very wicked and foolish."

"Along with every other member of the human family," he said. "I suppose God is repaying you for your wickedness?"

She nodded.

"Well," he said, wrapping an arm around her, "I don't think He's as cruel as all that. If you confess your faults to Him, He will forgive you."

"But the fruits of my folly remain," she said. "The trouble I have brought about remains."

"True," he said. "All choices have results, some good, some not so good."

"Mine have brought a whirlwind upon us."

"Reminds me of a certain master's mate I ran against in Tobago years back. Did I ever tell you about him?"

"No."

"He was a surly brute, and proud as a peacock, like that Capt. Dudley. Took it into his head to have my ivory cane for himself."

"The one with the silver handle?"

"Aye, given me by my father. That mate ran me up and down the rigging day and night in the foulest weather, hoping to see me swept overboard. In those days I was agile as a monkey, and his attempts to make me kill myself came to nothing. I knew what he was up to, and I confess I made great shows of skill just to anger him. By the time we reached Tobago he'd had his fill. He arranged with some native scum to murder me. I was chosen to deliver a message from the ship's captain to the governor of the island, and the master's mate plotted with his assassins to waylay me on my return. As I was leaving the ship, the mate made a great display of making amends by giving me his own hat, with a bold, feathered cockade on its peak. 'Twas by the hat my murderers were to know me. A shipmate alerted me to the plot at the foot of the gangplank, but too late. I had to deliver the captain's message."

"What did you do?"

"On the way to the governor's mansion I thought a lot about how I'd deliberately infuriated the master's mate, and I saw the terrible position in which I had put myself. I prayed very hard, Rachel, and repented of my arrogance. But still I had to deliver the message. And suddenly I realized a way to escape my dilemma."

"How?"

"I put myself in a place where my assailants did not expect me to be."

"I don't understand."

"The road to the governor's mansion was wide and well known to everyone," he said. "I made a great display of marching proudly up the street with my message pouch tucked under an arm and that fine hat sitting prettily upon my head. But on leaving the governor's mansion, I removed the hat and stole out by a side gate. I took the byways along the perimeter of the town and made it back to the ship as safely as the baby Moses in his basket."

"What happened?"

"The master's mate was furious when I returned his hat to him. He grabbed it and marched down the gangplank to learn what had become of his scheme. Wouldn't you know that his assassins were too lazy to do the job themselves. They hired some other wretches more despicable than they, and paid them with a bottle of rum, which was consumed while lying in wait for me. So down the street marches the Master's Mate, not knowing that his assassins will not recognize him, and wearing the very hat by which they are to know him."

"What became of him?"

"His hirelings were most efficient, even when drunk. I was appointed the master's mate for the return voyage. And the cane still belongs to me."

He took her hand.

"Rachel, some trouble's meant to bring about greater good," he said. " 'Tis true we're sinners, but not all our troubles are caused by our sins. And those that are, God can redeem. This tempest may be painful while you're walking through it, but afterward you will better understand what it is about."

"But my father," she said, "they may hang him."

"If it comes to that, your father's ready to meet his Maker, and we can be grateful for that. It can't be helped, Rachel. But as I think about this, it seems to me the redcoats are using him."

"Using him? Whatever for?"

"To ferret out the ghost."

"I don't understand."

" 'Tis a trap, lass, as plain as the nose on your face. They're wagering that Regina Silsby will come to fetch your father out."

"But suppose she cannot aid him."

"She shall think of a way," he said. "This Regina Silsby fellow is wonderfully clever, far more so than you or I. But to my way of thinking, all that's needed is for the ghost to put himself in a place where he's not expected to be."

"How will he manage that?"

"The redcoats claim your father is the ghost," he said. "They can't very well keep him locked in a prison if the ghost should suddenly appear somewhere else."

"You mean . . ."

"Go a'haunting where your father is not."

"Of course," she said, brightening, "what a marvelous idea. I'm sure Regina Silsby will think of it. He must think of it."

"And if I were he," Grandfather said, "I would make a great show of it. All Boston must witness it. Then these redcoats won't have a leg to stand on. They'll have to release your father."

"Oh, Grandfather, that is wonderful," she said. "Let us pray this very moment that God will guide Regina Silsby rightly."

They held hands and prayed. And as they prayed, her mind turned to Mr. Newcomb's steam invention. Over and over in her head spun the revolving drum. She saw the mist spewing from the spouts and the mechanical legs pumping the organ bellows. She remembered the organ's mighty blast, and suddenly her thoughts crystallized. Joy cascaded through her heart so strongly that laughter began to bubble from her lips.

"He has heard us," she said, tears moistening her cheeks. "The Lord has heard us."

"I believe He has," Grandfather said. "And I believe this Regina Silsby fellow will know exactly what's to be done."

"I believe so, too. Thank you, Grandfather."

She hugged him.

"Cheer up, lass," he said, rising. "Trust the Lord and see what He does."

"I shall."

He left the room and closed the door. Already Rachel's mind was whirling. There were many things to be done.

"And I must have a bath before I go out," she said.

Nineteen

The Recital

The night was black. Clouds heavy with sleet blotted out the moon. Winds howled, hurling pellets of ice down the streets.

Rachel's heart was laughing. On such a night she should be terrified, but this night she was exhilarated. She felt the presence of the Lord at her back and knew that her grandfather's advice was sound. Regina Silsby would show herself in the place where she was least expected, in the place where she had lived her last days, in the very place where she had died—the King's Chapel.

"Yea, the darkness hideth not from thee," she said aloud, quoting David's psalm. Other Bostonians might think this a horrid, heaven-forsaken evening, but not she. The Lord Himself

was in the terror, filling the darkness with His own awesome presence. As in Egypt on the Passover night, when the destroying angel smothered the land, so was Boston on this night. The Spirit of God was brooding over the earth, and all its inhabitants trembled.

Already masked, Rachel slunk toward the side wall of the chapel to the window she had unlocked before supper. Her wad of wax was still stuck in the window pane, holding shut the glass while keeping it unbolted. A sharp tug freed the window.

"There's a good lass," came a voice from the shadows. "Have you any comfort for a lost soul?"

From a dark doorway lurched a drunken man.

"The night's cold, lass," he said, grabbing her arm. "Let's have some warmth from you."

She snarled and pressed her withered face against his. The man dropped backward in a dead faint.

"Serves you right," she said while brushing off her sleeve. "You should be ashamed of yourself, preying upon helpless women such as I. Now, if you will excuse me."

She squeezed through the window and clamped it shut.

"Safe," she sighed. Hopefully the ruffian would be gone when she returned to the street.

She left her darkened lantern closed, fearing that someone outside might see its tiny glow through the windows. After letting her eyes adjust to the chapel's blackness, she made her way to the nave. Cruciforms and candlesticks she thrust through all the door handles, barring shut the entries. At the church's rear door she did the same. No one would be able to penetrate the chapel, even with a key. Satisfied that all was secured, she mounted the stairway to the loft. Ice was thick on the steps, just as on the night Regina Silsby had died. Rachel approached the organ and found Mr. Newcomb's steam apparatus as he had left it. He had added a funnel to one of the drum's hollow axles with a heavy lead ball acting as a stopper.

"Perfect," she said. Rolling the drum back and forth, she listened to the slosh within and gauged the kettle to be a quarter-full. She needed more water and fuel for a proper fire. Grabbing a pail from a corner, she retraced her steps to the window. Back outside she went, past the drunk still lying unconscious in the street, to a neighboring house's rain barrel. With the bucket she broke the barrel's ice and filled the pail with chilly water. Standing beneath the chapel window she realized she could not lift the bucket into the sanctuary without spilling it.

She thought a moment, then left the bucket by the wall and crawled back inside the chapel. The minister always belted his Sunday robes with an ornamental rope. It must be somewhere in the sacristy. By this time she was quite comfortable wandering about in the darkness. She located the room, searched its closets, and found what she wanted. Returning to the window, she dropped down to the street and knotted the rope around the bucket's handle.

"Firewood," she remembered aloud. Past the drunk she tramped again to the same neighbor's house.

" 'Tis for a noble cause," she said while helping herself to an armful of logs by the kitchen door. "My father and I thank you most sincerely."

While lugging the wood back to the chapel, she vowed to do something charitable for the homeowner, to repay him for his donation. She would replace the wood, of course, perhaps even leave a cranberry loaf or a kidney pie on the kitchen step—with a handwritten note of thanks from Regina Silsby!

On second thought, the note was best left undone. The household might suspect the treats were poisoned.

At the chapel wall she dropped her load and scrambled once more through the window. With the rope she hoisted up the water bucket and carried it to the organ loft. Using the organist's bench as a stool, she poured water into the funnel, listening as the liquid splashed into the kettle's belly. She stopped when the cauldron seemed half-full. Back downstairs and outside she went to lash the logs together with her rope and lift them through the window as well.

At last everything was ready. The doors were barred, the windows locked. The drum was half-filled with water, and the firewood arranged in the brazier. She paused for prayer.

"Unless the Lord builds the house," she said aloud, *"they labor in vain who build it.* Lord God, without You I cannot succeed, and with You I cannot fail. Whether my deeds are right or wrong I know not. I know only that my father's life is in danger because of me. Let me not labor in vain this night. If You know a better way, I pray You will show it to me."

She waited for some warning not to proceed. Sensing nothing, she touched a candle to her lantern, and with the taper kindled the fire. Tiny flames spread through the wood and slowly swelled into a blaze. The fire licked the belly of the kettle and cast an eerie glow across the loft. Shadows loomed everywhere, cavorting across the walls as the flames leapt and danced upon the brazier. The sanctuary seemed transformed into a hellish grotto. Dominating the expanse was the slumbering organ, its great rows of ivory teeth bared, its head bristling with hundreds of horns. At the beast's side squatted Mr. Newcomb's steam kitchen like a horrid, two-legged reptile. Kneeling before both monsters, tending her offerings of fire and water, was the ghost who would soon bring them to life.

Rachel stoked and stirred the fire, counting the minutes and wondering how long before the machine would be ready. She was grateful for the foul weather. It would keep the streets deserted, and thus prevent anyone from noticing the glow of her brazier in the chapel windows. If someone should see the light too soon and sound an alarm of fire, her plans would be ruined.

At last she heard gurgling and hissing within the cauldron. Boiling water began to bump and bang against the copper walls. Knocks became clatters. The gases within the kettle's belly roiled and sighed, and finally breathed their steam through the spouts. She watched intently as the mists strengthened into spitting clouds. The drum began to spin.

Another pair of logs brightened the fire. The steam kitchen's legs quickened their pace from a walk to a jog. Soon they were running wildly, filling the dragon's diaphragm with air. The great beast stirred, gathering its strength for a monstrous bellow. Rachel could feel the wind blowing through the instrument's bowels, waiting for release through its wind pipes. She sat in the maw of the giant, dwarfed by its body of silver, brass, lead, and wood.

By the light of the brazier she selected her stops for a grand performance. She had brought no hymnal, no music books, only Regina Silsby's score. From memory she would blend together everything she knew into a single, strange phantasm of sound.

"It is not too late to stop," she said as she spread her fingers over the keyboard. "Tell me now. There's no turning back, once I commit myself."

Silence.

"Very well," she said. "Shall we begin?"

After drawing a deep breath she thrust her fingers downward. The loft and rafters shuddered with a battle cry of a thousand voices. Trumpets, flutes, reeds, and basses boomed from the chapel tower and rolled across the rooftops of Boston. The sound rattled windows. Icicles trembled and snapped. Snow tumbled from roofs. Dogs barked. The ground quaked. Windows opened, and eyes followed the sound to the King's Chapel, where a light was glowing in the sanctuary windows.

Rachel's fingers danced across the organ's keys. Like a trained stallion the beast responded with melodious agility, traipsing through fanfares and chord strings, leaping from melody to melody, exultantly roaring its prowess. Within the chapel tower the great bells hummed in resonant harmony. The entire sanctuary reverberated with sound. Fast and furiously she played. Sweat was beading on her brow as she worked, driven, consumed, fused into a single spirit with her instrument.

Together rider and beast romped across their musical landscape. Rachel could not keep from bouncing upon the bench as her toes worked the bass pedals. Never had such exhilaration flooded through her. The choice to play her music was right and good. But not until she had committed herself had she known for certain.

She paused to blot the moisture from her brow. Torches shimmered outside the windows as townsfolk gathered in the street. An iron key jingled in the lock of the sanctuary door, but the candlesticks barring the handles held them closed.

"It won't open," someone shouted from outside. Rachel dismounted to pour more water into the kettle and stoke the fire. She jumped back upon the organ bench and spread before her the sheets of Regina Silsby's final piece. Someone in the crowd would surely remember her music. The melody would resurrect many memories and confirm the identity of the phantom.

She charged into the music with the same fervor that Regina Silsby had written into it. Her strange chords, exuberant rhythms, and fantastic melodies poured from the chapel into the streets. The sound of the great behemoth was far more glorious than anything the tiny clavichord could evoke. No wonder Regina Silsby had come to the chapel night after night. It was euphoric.

A window shattered. Crowds would soon be flooding the sanctuary. Rachel fought an urge to flee and continued playing. It wasn't enough that Regina Silsby be heard. She must be seen. Already there was shouting in the nave below. The chapel doors burst open. Footsteps stampeded into the sanctuary. A collective gasp from the floor below signaled the time to halt. Rachel turned about and gazed to the pavement below. Staring up at her were dozens of horrified citizens, many still in their nightshirts, with bare legs sticking out beneath tasseled fringes.

"Look!" one said, pointing to the choir loft.

"Regina Silsby."

In silence the ghoul and the mob stared at each other.

"Fetch her down," someone shouted. "She can't bewitch us all."

The crowd rushed the chapel stairwell. Rachel leapt from the bench and fled behind the organ. With a gasp she remembered the music sheets and returned for them. Men were slipping on the steps and tumbling back upon each other. The icy obstacle gave her the precious seconds she needed to retrieve the music and flee to the back of the organ box. She popped open a panel accessing the cavity behind the pipes, and squeezed inside, pulling shut the panel after her. Blinded by the darkness, she let her fingers guide her through the forest of pipes, until she had retreated to the farthest recess of the cavern. There she waited, heart pounding, lungs panting as she listened to the sounds beyond the wooden wall.

Into the organ loft poured the mob. At the sight of the racing machinery they slowed to a stop. The monstrous apparatus was spewing steam and flailing stout legs up and down. Its spinning belly glowed in flames.

"Witchery," someone said.

"The thing's alive. She's cast a spell upon it."

"Kill it."

With staves and clubs the mob battered Newcomb's machine apart. Water spilled from the kettle's bowels, dousing the fire. The legs splintered apart and the entire contraption collapsed in a crumpled heap.

"Where's the ghost?"

"Vanished."

"She must be here. She can't have escaped."

A scream from the opposite end of the chapel drew their attention across the sanctuary. Racing along the altar rail far below was the phantom, robed in black and cackling a wicked laugh. She turned her gruesome face toward them, hurled a horrific howl their way, and vanished past the rear entry.

"After her," someone said.

The mob tumbled downstairs and bounded toward the back of the church.

"The door's bolted."

"If she gets into her coffin, we'll never catch her."

Keys clattered. The door banged open and the crowd rushed outdoors.

Cautiously Rachel emerged from the organ box. The shattered remains of Mr. Newcomb's machine lay sprawled across the loft. Her heart sank, but she had no time to wallow in regret. Nor could she fathom what had happened in the sanctuary, or whose scream it was that had drawn the mob from the loft. The puzzle was dismissed for more pressing matters.

She descended the stairs. Most of the crowd, too timid to venture into the chapel, remained in the street. Across the sanctuary to the side window she crept and squeezed through to the pavement below. She left the pane swinging on its hinges and retreated down the street. Her drunken assailant still lay where he had fallen, snoring loudly. She scurried past him and vanished into an alley.

Not until she reached the back gate of her father's garden did she slow her pace. Through the shrubbery she bustled and climbed the woodpile to her window. Thrusting up the sash, she tumbled through the opening, gathered up her bed sheet ladder, and banged down the pane once more. After arranging the curtains she tugged off her wig and mask.

"Well, that's that," she said with a smile.

"Indeed?" came a voice from behind her. She spun around. Capt. Dudley sat in the corner chair.

"Don't look so shocked, child," he said. "I wanted an extra tot of rum and came to have you fetch it. When you didn't answer my knock I used a knife to lift the door latch. And what should I find but an empty room. Where, I wondered, could pretty Rachel be, this far into the night? And why this knotted bed sheet hanging from her window? When that ruckus at the King's Chapel started I decided to wait for you, Rachel Winslow . . . or is it Regina Silsby?"

He snatched the mask from her trembling hand.

"Clever," he said, studying it, "for such a common girl. Sergeant!"

Hodges appeared in the doorway.

"Fetch a guard here at once," Dudley said. "Arrest her."

Twenty
❧
Secrets Shared

Deep in the bowels of the Customs House, a cell door creaked open. Jeremiah Winslow sat up and squinted into a bright lantern.

"You are at liberty to go," a guard told him.

"Have you caught the scoundrel?" Winslow said, shielding his eyes.

"Only last night," the guard said.

"I hope he gets what's coming to him."

"Be sure of that."

Winslow rose to his feet. The cold, the damp, and the hours of inactivity had stiffened his body, and with awkward strokes he brushed the straw from his coat. The guard led him through the cellar and up the stairs to the marble rotunda. Capt. Dudley met him at the outer door.

"Well, Winslow," Dudley said, "you don't seem any worse for wear."

"I'm told you captured the rogue, my lord."

"Red-handed."

"My congratulations to you. I trust you've planned a proper punishment for him."

"Indeed," Dudley said. "It appears we were entirely mistaken about you."

"Then I shall take my leave of you, my lord."

"You may, and a very good day to you. Don't expect to see me at your house until the morrow. I've much to attend to here."

With a nod Winslow descended the marble steps to the street. The captain seemed strangely gleeful about his conquest, but Winslow dismissed the observation. His stomach was growling, and his tongue was parched. Unshaved stubble bristled on his cheeks, and his disheveled clothes and hatless brow brought stares from passersby. Stiffly he marched the crowded streets toward home, and at last stumbled through his own doorway.

"Jeremiah," his wife said from the hall. "You've come home. Thank heaven."

She wrapped her arms around him and kissed his dirty cheeks.

"You must be famished," she said.

"And cold."

"Rachel," Mrs. Winslow said. "Your father's come back. Rachel."

She peeled off her husband's coat and ushered him to the hearth.

"I'll have soup and ale for you straightaway," she said. "You must warm yourself."

Grandfather wandered into the parlor.

"They let you out," he said.

"Aye," Winslow said. "The scoundrel's been caught."

"Regina Silsby?"

"High time too. I was getting stiff and cold."

Grandfather turned white.

"You're quite certain she's been captured?" he said.

"They took her last night."

Grandfather rushed from the room and mounted the stairs.

"Rachel," he said.

Mrs. Winslow returned to the room with a mug of hot ale.

"What's got into him?" she said.

"I told him they had captured Regina Silsby," Winslow said, "and he's off in a mad search for Rachel."

"Regina Silsby? They've taken her?"

"After that strange business last night at the King's Chapel, I expect. Did you hear the music?"

"All Boston must have," she said. "Everyone is talking about it. They say Regina Silsby was playing at the chapel organ. How ghastly. It reminds me of . . ."

She shook away the memory. Grandfather descended the stairs.

"Has anyone checked the barn?" he said.

"I have just come from there," Mrs. Winslow said.

"Then Rachel's gone."

"Where?" Winslow said.

"To the Customs House, I suppose."

"Whatever for?"

"Confound it, man," Grandfather said. " 'Tis your own daughter they've arrested."

"What?"

"Rachel is Regina Silsby."

"Are you mad?" Winslow said.

"By thunder, I ought to know," Grandfather said. "I've been following her from the start."

Winslow blinked, stupefied.

"I saw her," Grandfather said, "coming home after that first stint at the Green Dragon, but didn't make much of it. The next night she's out again, and Regina Silsby's seen that very evening. I spied her climbing the wood stack to her chamber window. 'That's odd,' says I. 'Why would Rachel be roaming about in the middle of the night?' 'Twas from the graveyard she came, and through my spyglass I spotted a horse munching the grass at Regina Silsby's grave, with a regimental saddle on its back. 'Blow me down,' says I, ' 'Tis my little Rachel that's Regina Silsby.' So I donned a cloak and started following her after that. Every time she slipped from the house, I tagged along. I followed her to the Customs House, where she freed old Gray from the pillory and raised such a ruckus aboard the *Devonshire*."

"Rachel?" Winslow said. "My Rachel?"

"Aye, your Rachel. All by herself she crossed the harbor. I rowed out after her, and while she was aboard ship I cut the anchor cables, just to distract the crew a wee bit. She'd have caught her death of cold, too, if I hadn't ferried her back here after the deed was done. Last night she was out again at the King's Chapel. I followed her there too and got her out of a pickle, if I say so myself. She staged her little performance to rescue you."

"Performance?"

"You heard the organ last night, did you not?"

"I did."

" 'Twas Rachel making the ghost appear somewhere that you were not. That's how she proved you were not Regina Silsby. And now they've caught her, they have."

Mr. and Mrs. Winslow sat dumbstruck.

"This is impossible," Winslow said.

"Search the house," Grandfather said. "Search the grounds, search the garden. Search everywhere. You won't find her. She's in the Customs House cellar, and only God knows their plans for her."

Winslow could only gape in amazement.

"What are we to do?" he said. Grandfather tossed a leather mask into Winslow's lap.

"Fetch her out, I suppose," he said.

Twenty-one

❦

Reactions

Mr. Newcomb tramped the cobbled lane to Josiah Sinquin's shop. So hard did he thrust open the door that the copper bell snapped from its spring. The clatter startled Sinquin and Wyeth, who spilled their toddies into the hearth. Robert stood by the workbench, fanning the coals beneath the crucible. Newcomb stared wildly about the room.

"I know who is Regina Silsby," he said. Sinquin and Wyeth jumped to their feet.

"What's that you say?" Sinquin said.

"Regina Silsby," Newcomb said. "The redcoats arrested her last night. Oh, it is horrible."

"Well, who is she?" Sinquin said. "Speak up, man."

"Rachel Winslow."

Robert's jaw dropped. Sinquin and Wyeth gaped at each other, then howled with laughter.

"Pretty Rachel Winslow?" Sinquin said. "Old fellow, your jest is too preposterous. You nearly stopped my heart with it."

" 'Tis no jest," Newcomb said. "The ghost cannot be anyone else."

"Do you expect us to believe," Sinquin said, "that a simple-minded girl has thrown all Boston into a frenzy?"

"The music she played last night. Did you hear it?"

"At the King's Chapel? Who did not hear it? Upon my word, sir. Just because Rachel Winslow can play the organ—"

" 'Tis not so simple as that," Newcomb said. "I gave her a sheaf of music and asked her to learn it for me. There's not another copy of it in the world. 'Twas that very piece the ghost played last night. And my steam invention. Rachel is the only person who knew how to work it. That's how she pumped the organ bellows."

"What steam invention?"

"I constructed a machine to power the organ."

"And Rachel knew how to work it?"

"I showed her," Newcomb said. " 'Twas a secret between us."

"Where is this secret invention?"

"Gone," Newcomb said, "destroyed last night by the mob."

"You're mad, sir. Even if you could create such a device, I doubt that pretty Rachel would have the wit to—"

"She's a clever one," Newcomb said, "far more clever than either of you, that I can see. And my steam invention was real, I saw it work. 'Twas glorious. I took a lesson from the ancient Greeks, you see—calculated that the steam of boiling water, when directed through a narrow tube, would create a blast strong enough to . . ."

"Aye," Sinquin said, stifling a yawn, "doubtless your device was a wonder. Who else has seen it?"

"Rachel, of course, and my son, Thaddeus."

"A very reliable pair of witnesses."

"Confound the both of you," Newcomb said. "We've got to help her. Call up the Sons of Liberty at once."

"Whatever for?"

"Why, to free her, of course. The redcoats are holding her at the Customs House."

"How do you know this?"

"I heard two grenadiers boasting of it this morning."

"They won't jail a woman," Sinquin said.

"They will," Newcomb said, "and they have. That Capt. Dudley's got it in for her, that's what the soldiers said. If you won't help her, I shall seek assistance elsewhere. I shall go to Sam Adams myself."

"No need for that," Sinquin said. "Robert, get yourself down to the Customs House and see if your sister's imprisoned there. No, on second thought I shall go myself."

He jammed his hat on his head and wrapped his cloak about him. Wyeth and Newcomb followed him into the snow. The door banged shut.

Robert stared after them. How could Newcomb's tidings be true? Rachel was a girl, modest and temperate, given to washing and baking and sewing. Who would mistake her for a rogue as bold and cunning as Regina Silsby? All Boston was gabbing how the ghost had pinned Capt. Dudley's hat to the Devonshire's mast and felled half the ship's crew with her knives. Rachel could not even throw a dagger. Nor had she the courage to roam about Boston in the dead of night.

He pumped the leather bellows and the furnace coals flared. Images flooded his mind of Rachel dressed in men's clothing, scrambling up the rigging of their father's ships. Her favorite perch was the tip of the bowsprit, where the ocean swells would heave her toward the sky, then plunge her into roiling troughs. How she would laugh as the waves split beneath her. She had mastered compass and sextant, something he had never managed to do. She could chart a course, read the skies, and gauge the weather. Clever indeed she was, and daring as well. But clever and daring enough to masquerade as Regina Silsby?

She was far too pretty to be taken for the ghoul that had terrorized Boston Neck and the Green Dragon. With a shudder he recalled the phantom's gruesome face. Not even a blind man could mistake his sister for the ghost. Unless . . .

His cheeks went sallow. Had she somehow disguised her face? It seemed impossible. But she had been clever enough to learn of the Pembroke raid, and the ghost had magically arrived at Boston Neck to stop it. There was no denying that Rachel could play the organ, as the ghost had done on the previous night. Somehow she must have taught herself how to throw a knife as well. However impossible, the conclusion was inescapable.

He paced the shop, wondering what to do, and dreading that whatever he did would bring a beating. At last his concern for his sister conquered his fear for himself. He doused the furnace's flame and grabbed his hat and coat. Leaving the shop door swinging on its hinges, he rushed into the street, uncertain where to go. Someone must be told what he knew. But who?

❧

In the tiny Customs House office, Dudley stood stiffly before Col. Leslie.

"Wonderful," Leslie shouted, "truly marvelous, Captain. I send you searching for a traitor, and you bring me a child."

"She is the ghost," Dudley said. "It can be proved."

"Blast you for a simpleton," Leslie said. "What am I to do? Hang her as a spy? Have her shot perhaps? Or flog her 'round the fleet?"

"She was caught," Dudley said, "escaping from the King's Chapel—in the very act, my lord."

"And how will the citizens of Boston react, Captain, when they learn we've accused a girl of confounding the British army and navy? Have you considered that?"

"In truth, my lord, I . . ."

"Set us up for laughing stocks is what you've done. And if we attempt to punish her, every colony in America will hate us ten times more than they do now. I daresay even the hounds will begin biting us as we pass. You've outdone yourself, sir. Thanks to you, we must appear either as fools or as demons. I certainly do not want to show myself the latter."

He dropped into his desk chair and began scribbling orders.

"We shall let her go quietly," he said, "with strict warnings not to haunt the streets of Boston again."

"Am I to understand," Dudley said, "that his lordship will do nothing?"

"You understand correctly, Captain. Perhaps there's a brain in that thick skull of yours after all."

"May I remind my lord," Dudley said, "that the prisoner has aided in the desertion of impressed seamen and in the escape of a jailed prisoner. She has given sanctuary to enemies of the crown, to say nothing of running the *Devonshire* aground and nearly burning her to cinders. These are capital offenses, my lord. I hardly think a warning, however strict, is sufficient."

"You don't think at all, Captain, that's your problem. What should be her punishment? Answer me that."

"The code is very clear, my lord."

"Indeed. And how do you propose we answer the citizens' outrage when we carry out her sentence?"

"Why concern ourselves with them at all, my lord? They are commoners."

"The world is changing, Dudley. Get used to it. We can't run roughshod over these people, not as before. Had we learned that lesson sooner, we'd not be in our present predicament. Do you realize that these commoners, as you call them, outnumber us a hundred or more to one, and that many of them are armed as well or better than we? If it comes to blows, they'll bloody us, sir, and they may bloody us badly."

"My lord is surprisingly pessimistic."

"You would do well to get off that aristocratic hobby horse of yours," Leslie said, "and look about you. Daily their militias drill on the common, and nightly their mobs rule the streets. When we rise to confront them, they vanish into a thousand homes."

"My lord, if laws are broken, culprits must be punished. Peasants who rise up against their masters must be crushed."

"What do you suggest, Captain? Should we burn entire villages and slaughter whole communities? Shall we crucify them along the highways, as the Romans did? The principle works both ways. If we oppress these people, if we misuse our authority over them, we rightly earn their contempt, and they will sooner or later rise up against us, and may overwhelm us."

"They are peasants, my lord."

"As were your ancestors, Captain, and mine. Nothing is secure, sir. A brief examination of English history should tell you that. Crowns and titles do not last to all generations, and today's peasants are tomorrow's princes. If we behave too arrogantly amongst these people, we shall fall, and they shall rise to replace us."

"This is coward's talk," Dudley said. "Until now, I regarded my lord with utmost respect. That, I confess, is altered. It appears that you haven't the backbone to command troops, or to rule peoples."

"And you have?"

"This girl must be made an example," Dudley said. "Those who defy the king must suffer the consequences. If you fail to fulfill your duty to king and country, you are not fit to wear his majesty's uniform."

The two men glowered at each other.

"I shall choose to overlook your insubordination," Leslie said. "You are still under my command, and my orders are that nothing is to be done against this girl. Whoever does so answers to me. Is that understood?"

"Perfectly."

Twenty-two

✠

Imprisoned

Rachel sat on the stone floor of her cell. The chains about her wrists and ankles rattled whenever she moved. Although hunger and fatigue plagued her, fear did not. She had endured too many escapades for that. Nor was she sorry for what she had done. Her actions were right, and she was ready to taste the fruit of them, however bitter. If anything, she was relieved. Her father would not suffer for her deeds.

Somehow she sensed that her punishment would be mild. While Capt. Dudley was an ogre, Col. Leslie was not. And since the colonel was acting governor of Massachusetts, as well as Dudley's superior officer, he would decide her punishment. Beyond his prescribed penance waited home and family.

How long before her mother and father realized what had befallen her? Who besides Dudley and his soldiers knew of her arrest? Days might pass before anyone found her. Would she starve before then? At least the cell was warm. Behind the brick wall at her back must be a hearth and fire, for the stones were warm.

She marveled at how stunned the soldiers had been to learn that Regina Silsby was a girl. Those who did not think her a genuine ghost had expected a man. That a girl could possess such audacious courage astounded them. Every few minutes another disbelieving face would appear at the barred window of her cell door.

"She's not really the ghost, is she?" the face would ask. "Incredible."

"You, girl. Prove to us that you are Regina Silsby. Show us some trick of yours."

Not a word did she answer. She was beginning to understand God's preference for humility over arrogance. The proud either laughed in derision or mocked her, hoping to regain some of their lost dignity. Others refused to believe she was the phantom at all.

"That's not Regina Silsby," they would say. "How could such a winsome thing outfox five hundred sailors, or terrify an entire regiment?"

"If you're Regina Silsby, prove yourself," others would demand. "Cast a witch's spell for us. Make some feat of magic."

She did nothing. Her challengers left grumbling that she deserved her fate. Only a few were willing to admit she had outwitted them.

"I must say, girl," one such said to her, "my hat's off to you. 'Twas a dreadful fright you gave me."

"I am sorry," she said. He and others like him were the only ones to whom she spoke.

Sometimes when she was alone she would slip from her pocket Regina Silsby's manuscript. The light was too dim to read the music well. She would refold the paper and return it to her skirt, only to retrieve and inspect it again. That one so gifted as Regina Silsby had died so young, that a single song was all that remained of her life, saddened her. She considered her own uncertain future and consoled herself by remembering that in God nothing was lost. His ways were indeed confusing but not so tangled as the plights into which His children plunged themselves.

During the many hours of solitude, she prayed.

"Thank You, Father, for being near to me," she would say, sensing His presence, glad that He had not abandoned her despite her follies. "Whatever fate You have for me, I accept."

She pondered how grand was the reputation of the ghost, and how modest was the girl behind the mask. Regina Silsby was a spirit of awesome prowess and power, a terror to oppressors, a cunning and courageous rogue. Rachel Winslow was the daughter of a shipmaster who did not believe in pampering his children. She cooked meals, washed clothes, tended animals, scrubbed floors. She was hardly better than a kitchen maid. Yet she and Regina Silsby were the same.

It was then she realized that Jesus Christ was the person masking the face of God Almighty. Jesus had no grace or beauty to admire. He was despised by men, rejected, and not esteemed. Yet Jesus and God were the same person. The Almighty had hidden Himself in the man and had walked amidst His creation. *"He came unto His own,"* John's gospel said, *"and His own received Him not."* Some derided Him; many despised Him. To the few who recognized Him and believed in Him, He granted an inheritance in His heavenly kingdom.

"Hah, well met," said a voice beyond the wall. "What news have you?"

Rachel could not tell if the sound was above or beside her chamber, but the voice was Capt. Dudley's.

"I'm told my lord has captured the ghost, Regina Silsby," said a second voice. It sounded familiar, but she could not place it.

"They say it is a common girl you've arrested," the newcomer said.

"Just so," Dudley said, "and no thanks to you for any part of it."

" 'Tis true, then? The one accused is Rachel Winslow?"

"I caught her myself, returning to her house from the King's Chapel haunting."

A chair creaked. The stranger must have dropped into it.

"You were no use at all in catching her," Dudley said. "Heaven knows why I pay you so much. 'Twas more than a fortnight ago you brought me any news of value. I thought these Sons of Liberty trusted you."

"They do, my lord."

She gasped. The Sons of Liberty had a spy among them.

"No matter," Dudley went on. "I've got her now, and I'll have no trouble disposing of her."

"Indeed, my lord?"

" 'Tis all over town she's a witch," Dudley said. "There's neighbors who'll testify that she's been brewing evil broths in her father's barn, cavorting about undressed at all hours and even washing herself in the vile potions. Only last night she was making black magic in the King's Chapel. Half of Boston witnessed that profanity. Did you hear of the infernal machine she raised to life by her sorcery? I'm told it was possessed of a demon spirit and running all about the choir loft on its own. Who knows what other hellish evil she's been about? 'Tis tragic, my good friend. That pretty wench is a witch most foul."

"Surely my lord cannot believe such nonsense."

"What does it matter?" Dudley said. "The liberty-loving Boston rabble will believe it. 'Tis all I need."

"May I be permitted to see the prisoner, my lord?"

"With pleasure. Guard, escort my guest to the ghost. He may tarry five minutes."

Chairs scraped the floor above, and footsteps tramped overhead. Soon the noises were descending a nearby stairwell and pacing the grotto outside her cell. The door creaked open. Into the chamber stepped Josiah Sinquin.

"You!" she said

"What kind of greeting is that?" he said. "I've come to free you. I should think you would offer me a kiss."

"I would rather spit in your face," she said.

"What's come over you, Rachel? Is that any way to address your future husband? You know that I have spoken to your father."

"I hope he trounced you out of the house on your backside."

"Quite the contrary. One look at those emeralds had him eating from my hand. And so shall you, after I've delivered you from this prison."

"I'll die first," she said. "Traitor, Judas! Would you betray your own brethren?"

"Whatever do you mean?" he said.

"The Sons of Liberty," she said. "I have seen you sup with them. Yet you give them over to their enemies."

"I sup with anyone useful to me," he said. "My friends are those with money. Come, Rachel, don't be so naive."

"Tell me true. Who is your master, the Sons of Liberty, or the British?"

"My master is whoever pays me most," he said. "I tell the Sons of Liberty what the lobster-backs are doing, and I tell the lobster-backs what the Sons of Liberty are doing. I am a friend to both sides, and both sides pay me well."

"You are a black-hearted rogue."

"I am practical," he said, "a man of business. Don't you see, Rachel? Whoever wins is my friend. I take the surest route, the wisest route."

"The odious route," she said. "I can respect the British because they revere their king. The patriots I admire because they are loyal to each other and to their cause. But you are loyal only to yourself."

"There is no better cause than one's own."

"You disgust me."

"Choose your words more carefully, Rachel. I can free you."

"At what price? Must I promise to become your bride and trade this jail for a worse one?"

"My dear child, you talk as though I were a pauper."

"I care not a whit whether you are rich or poor. There is more to a man than mere money."

"Who else has come to see you besides myself? Anyone? Even your family and friends have abandoned you, but I shall not. When I've married you, your reputation shall be completely restored. All this ill will is unnecessary. I have influence with Capt. Dudley. A good word or two from me, and—"

"Do not waste your breath," she said. "I despise you. I rue the day you were born. Be gone from me."

"Every girl in Boston would be glad to be my wife," he said. "But I've chosen none of them. 'Tis you I want at my side, Rachel. I should expect you to be more grateful."

"A lovers' quarrel, have we?" Dudley said from the cell doorway. Rachel turned her back on him.

"Dear, dear," Dudley said. "Well, Sinquin, if it's her freedom you're after, I'm afraid her crimes are too high for that. She cannot be released."

"What's to become with her?"

"My dear fellow, she's to be hanged in the morning."

"Impossible."

"Spies and traitors are always treated thus. Ghosts get even worse."

"But she is just a girl," Sinquin said. "She could not possibly understand the nature of her actions."

"I'm afraid there's nothing to be done."

"But why such haste, my lord?"

" 'Tis the only time I've got," Dudley said. "Col. Leslie will be abroad at Castle Island tomorrow, so I must move quickly. He's got no stomach for this sort of thing. But once the deed's done, he'll see the wisdom of it."

"My lord!"

"Really, Sinquin, you are becoming tiresome. But I suppose I might be persuaded to be lenient."

"How so, my lord? Whatever you wish, I shall do."

"My, my," Dudley said. "There's more to you than money, after all. How very refreshing."

"Tell me what you want."

"The Sons of Liberty," Dudley said, "every last one of them. Deliver them all to me on the morrow, and I'll exchange their lives for hers."

"By my faith," Sinquin said. "How can I manage such a thing?"

"They trust you," Dudley said. "You told me so yourself. Surely you can think of some way to accomplish it. A rescue, perhaps."

"My lord?"

"Arrange a rescue of the wench there. By heaven, there's a fine idea. I shall run her down to the gallows at Boston Neck, and on the way your precious Sons of Liberty will come rushing into the waiting arms of my grenadiers."

Sinquin struggled with his warring emotions. Dudley's demand was difficult on such short notice, but Rachel's gratitude would be boundless.

"It shall be done, my lord," he said. "When I learn the details, I shall bring them to you, even to the signals of the leaders."

"By Jove, that would be worth her life. And you shall have her, if your word is good."

"It is, my lord."

Twenty-three

✤

The Gallows

Rachel's cell was dark when the barred door screeched open. A soldier held up a lantern.

"Get up," he said, prodding her with his boot. She stretched her stiff limbs.

"On your feet," he said. After loosening her chains he tugged her arms behind her back. With a rope he bound her wrists.

"Does Col. Leslie know of this?" she said.

"You hear that, lads?" he said to his comrades in the hall. "She wants the colonel."

"He's on Castle Island until the morrow," they said, "and by then she'll not need him."

"He'll not be pleased with this," she said.

"What does it matter to you, *Regina Silsby*? You'll not escape this time."

The soldier shoved her toward the doorway, and six others led her outside. Fog shrouded the Customs House square, where two rows of grenadiers lined the pavement, their scarlet coats spattered with drizzling rain. At the base of the stone steps Capt. Dudley sat atop his horse, a gloved fist planted on his hip. Beside him waited a two-wheeled cart drawn by a swaybacked nag. Rachel's escorts led her down the marble steps and lifted her into the cart. Her hands were lashed to one of the wagon's rails.

"Is this your doing?" she said to Dudley. "Or has Col. Leslie ordered me treated thus?"

"The colonel is too much a gentleman for this sort of thing," he said. "He'll learn of our little jaunt on the morrow."

"You intend to bait the Sons of Liberty," she said, "by parading me through the streets."

"To Boston Neck, actually. You're to be executed, as you well know. But I hear rumors that the Sons of Liberty shall attempt a rescue. How unfortunate that they shan't succeed."

"I could call out a warning."

"Aye, so you could. But I've already taken precautions against it. Private, muzzle this sow."

A soldier mounted the cart and knotted a kerchief around her mouth. She shrieked, but the cloth garbled her cries.

"Heavens, child," Dudley said. "You'll have to speak more clearly than that. I cannot understand a word you're saying. By Jove, men, listen to her drivel. Wouldn't you say she sounds much like the pig she is?"

Laughter sounded down the lines. Dudley allowed himself a satisfied smile before nodding to a nearby sergeant.

"Shoulder arms," the sergeant barked. Muskets snapped upward.

"To the left, face. Right column, forward march."

A crimson line filed out of the square, black boots thumping the cobbles. Behind rumbled the cart, and the remaining column tramped after it.

From an adjoining byway the night watchman pondered the parade. At his side stood Rachel's brother Robert.

"You see?" Robert said. "It is just as I told you. Mr. Sinquin's in league with that redcoat captain there. He's betrayed the Sons of Liberty to the lobster-backs."

Dudley spotted the pair.

"Seize those two," he said.

The watchman bolted, and Robert sprinted after him. Four soldiers peeled away from the column and pursued them.

Ahead of the soldiers ran a painted Indian wearing a tattered blanket. He darted into an alley.

"They're coming," he told a second warrior.

"How many?"

"Two dozen."

"Muskets?"

"Loaded with powder and ball."

"The lads won't like that. Is she among them?"

"Bound up like a witch to be burned. They mean to hang her at Boston Neck without a trial. 'Tis just as Sinquin told us."

"How he learned of it I shall never know. Alert the others. Do you remember the signal?"

"When the owl hoots and the two cocks crow."

"Aye. To Boston Neck then. Long life to the Sons of Liberty."

"Godspeed, friend."

They vanished in opposite directions.

The tramp of soldiers' boots brought early risers to their windows. Stares gave way to shouts.

"Ho, there, lobsterback. Where are you taking that lass? What's the crime?"

"By my soul. 'Tis a girl they've got."

"You don't mean the witch?"

"I know that girl. She's no sorceress."

Men gathered in the streets while women and children watched from their houses.

"What's to be done with her?" came shouts from the gathering mob.

"There's been no trial," others said. "Murder, that's what they're about."

"Men of Boston, are we to let this injustice stand?"

"No! Down with the red devils."

The crowd swelled into a throng as it converged on the town gate. Armed guards blocked the parade.

"Who goes there?" a sentry said. Dudley spurred his horse to the head of the crimson column.

"I am Thomas Dudley, son of the Earl of Leicester and captain of his majesty's 64th Regiment of Foot. Give me passage."

"By your command, my lord," the sentry said, stepping aside.

"Forward the prisoner," Dudley said. "Keep those ruffians back. Let no one follow us onto the Neck."

From a nearby rooftop an owl hooted. Two roosters crowed. Before their cries died away a horde of shrieking Indians exploded from the alleys. Rotting meat and vegetables splattered the soldiers.

"Death to tyranny," the savages shouted, waving staves and clubs.

" 'Tis the Sons of Liberty," Dudley said. "Enclose the wagon. Get the prisoner through the gate. Quick march."

Indians collided with the scarlet ranks. Flailing clubs felled soldiers. The cart rolled beneath the brick tunnel while crazed savages leapt upon its rails, knives flashing to cut Rachel's cords. Grenadiers dragged the warriors aside.

"Fix bayonets," Dudley said. "Skewer anyone who approaches the wagon."

"Get their muskets," said an Indian chief. "They can't stop all of us."

More soldiers collapsed. With his sword Dudley slashed at the painted warriors engulfing him. From a breast pocket he drew a silver bosun's whistle, pressed it to his lips and blew a shrill blast.

Drums thundered behind the houses. Fresh grenadiers rushed from barns and carriage houses, bayonets gleaming on the tips of their muskets. Rank upon rank of scarlet troops surrounded the throng, trapping citizens and Indians in a ring of sharpened steel.

Abruptly the drums ceased. Silence engulfed the square, broken only by the flap of regimental flags.

"Sons of Liberty," Dudley said. "Throw down your arms. Surrender now, or your wives shall all be widows this evening."

Stupefied Indians and citizens gaped at the red wall enclosing them.

"You call yourselves patriots?" Dudley shouted. "Cowards and traitors is what you are. Disarm at once, or I shall order you shot like dogs."

"But my lord," a sergeant said, "there are innocent citizens among them."

"You will shoot every man of them, if I so command," Dudley said. "Sons of Liberty, disarm. I shall not ask again."

Grimly the soldiers peered down their muskets at the rabble crowding the square. The trapped men exchanged dumbfounded glances.

A tremor shook the cobbles. Through the fog exploded a tidal wave of stampeding men. Short and tall, slender and stout, young and old, wealthy and wanting, they surged toward the gate like a raging flood. Hatless, coatless, some shoeless, every one of them carried a long rifle, powder horn and cartridge pouch. At the head of the multitude huffed the night watchman. Robert ran alongside him.

"Boston militia, surround the square," shouted the watchman. "Company A, to the left, Company B, to the right."

The horde parted behind him and bounded into the alleys at the soldiers' backs. Rifle muzzles were soon protruding from every window, corner, wagon, and post. A clatter of cocking hammers filled the square.

Dudley prodded the nag's rump with his sword.

"Through the gate, through the gate," he said. The cart trundled forward. He ducked into the tunnel, and a handful of soldiers squeezed after him. The gate slammed shut behind them.

"Grenadiers," came a command through the stout timbers. "About face. Present your arms."

"Boston militia, take aim. Shoot the officers first. Fire only on my order."

"Sons of Liberty, get the redcoats' muskets."

Indian war cries erupted anew, and clubs began clanging against steel. A great shout ascended from the square as citizens joined the fray.

Dudley listened calmly to the commotion. He slipped a snuff box from his pocket, drew a pinch between his thumb and forefinger, and sniffed the powder into his nostrils.

"Company," he said quietly, "proceed."

The soldiers advanced with the cart along the muddy stretch of Boston Neck. Fog rolled thick across the highway, swallowing the graveyard and the gibbets. At the gallows the parade halted. Dudley urged his horse to Rachel's side.

"I suppose," he said, "it should be obvious, even to you, that you'll hang despite my promise to Sinquin."

She glared at him.

"By nightfall you will be in your grave," he said. "Regina Silsby shall be no more, and the Sons of Liberty shall be in irons. What do you suppose Col. Leslie will say of that?"

She could only gape in horror.

"What's the matter, girl?" he said. "Cat got your tongue? Oh, dear, that silly rag is stopping you up. How inconvenient."

He shoved a knife behind her ear and severed the cloth. She spit the fabric from her mouth.

"I do hope," Dudley said, "you'll not waste your last words pleading for your life or the lives of those wretches back there. Not that I expect any of them to die with you. They will probably swear allegiance to their king and run home with their tails between their legs. Poltroon scum is all they really are—like you. This liberty nonsense will die a dog's death today."

"Will you not even permit me to bid farewell to my mother and father?" she said.

"Your parents shall learn your fate," he said, "when I deliver your carcass to them in a pine box. Should your father complain, I'll issue Writs of Assistance on all his ships and see him die a pauper. I may do that anyway. You've caused me a great deal of trouble, girl, and no small embarrassment. Let this be a lesson to you, and to every peasant who crosses me."

"Did you hear that?" said a masked phantom among the graves. The voice belonged to Rachel's grandfather.

"Scoundrel," said his hooded companion. "If that blackguard harms one hair on my daughter's head . . ."

"Patience, man, patience," Grandfather said. "Vengeance belongs to the Lord. Ours is but to rescue a brave soul. How's your wick?"

"Still lit," Winslow said.

"Pistols?"

"Primed and ready. But I have not shot in many a year, and this mask will surely spoil my aim."

"How many soldiers came through the gate?"

"Six, I think, plus his lordship. Hard to tell in this fog."

"I counted six as well. You know what to do?"

"As though my life depended on it."

"I'll not be long," Grandfather said. "Wait here for my signal."

He patted Winslow's shoulder and dissolved into the mist. Winslow fidgeted with the smoldering wick in his hand, watching the soldiers lift Rachel from the cart. They stood her before the gallows' wooden stair.

"The prisoner will mount the scaffold," Dudley said.

"And if I refuse?" she said.

"We've no use for your peasant gallantry, girl. Grenadiers, drag her up there."

"Boston militia," said a gruff voice from the fog at the water's edge. "Ready on the left flank."

"By my faith," a soldier said. "How did they get through the gate?"

His fellows glanced about, bewildered. There was no sergeant to direct them.

"Company," Dudley said. "Form up along the gallows. You, there. Lash her to the post and line up with the rest."

Five grenadiers stood shoulder to shoulder behind the platform. The sixth tied Rachel to the scaffold and joined them.

"Boston militia," said the voice in the fog. "Take aim."

"Company, present your arms," Dudley said. The soldiers leveled their muskets.

"Boston militia, ready and fire."

Flashes and thunderclaps rippled through the mist. Not one soldier fell.

"Grenadiers, return fire," Dudley said. "Shoot where the muzzle flames appeared."

The soldiers blasted blindly into the fog.

"Fix bayonets," Dudley said. "Prepare to charge the left bank."

Steel pikes were clamped to muskets.

"On my command," Dudley said. "Advance."

Into the fog the soldiers plunged, Dudley cantering alongside them. Ice and frozen earth shattered beneath them, hurling fragments about their legs. Across a bog strewn with dead men's bones the soldiers slogged. In the mud at the water's edge they slowed to a halt.

"Saints alive," a soldier said. "No one's here."

"They can't have dispersed that quickly," Dudley said.

"Spirits," another soldier said. "There's legions of them here."

"A ghost in every grave."

"Hold your tongues," Dudley said.

From his perch on the opposite shore Winslow heard a shrill whistle—Grandfather's signal. Quickly he said, "Boston militia, ready on the right flank."

He touched his wick to the fuse before him. A fiery trail slithered across the snow.

From the fog on the opposite shore Dudley shouted, "Company, about face. About face, you louts. Prepare to charge the right bank."

"Boston militia," Winslow said, "take aim."

His flame reached the first of his fused charges.

"On my command," he yelled. "Fire."

Shots erupted along the shoreline.

"Charge the right bank," Dudley said. Winslow scrambled into the mist along the water's edge. He was circling across the highway when the soldiers tumbled past him.

🌿

Rachel watched in complete confusion. Dudley and his soldiers raced first to one shore, then to the other. In the fog it was impossible to tell how many guns bristled on Boston Neck.

"Cambridge Militia," came a shout from the distant roadway. "Ready on the center. Take aim."

"Form up, form up," Dudley said through the mist. "Prepare to charge the road."

"Militia, on my command, fire."

Gunshots exploded in the highway.

"Grenadiers, advance," Dudley shouted, cantering toward the flashes. His men dashed after him.

"Retreat, retreat," the militia's commander said. "Fall back to the mainland."

The soldiers vanished in pursuit, leaving Rachel alone. A ghoul with a rotting face appeared at her side. Before she could shriek, the phantom slit her bindings.

"Not to worry, lass," he said. "Let's be off."

"Grandfather," she said.

"Hush, child. Come along, we've a skiff waiting for you."

He hurried her across the frozen earth.

"How many of you are there?" she said.

"Just your father and myself."

"Only two? How did you manage to—"

"Time a'plenty for stories later, child. Right now we've got to shove off before—"

Hooves pounded the earth. Through the fog careened a foaming stallion. Capt. Dudley straddled the beast's back, his saber slicing the air. Grandfather yanked a cutlass from his belt and blocked Dudley's blade.

"Rachel, get to the boat," Grandfather yelled. He shoved her toward the shore as Dudley rained blows on him. She stumbled and fell. Grandfather retreated between the legs of the scaffold, and Dudley spurred his mount around the structure.

"Grenadiers," Dudley said. "Here, by the gallows. I have them."

Helplessly Rachel watched her grandfather dodge Dudley's thrusts. Beyond the captain's prancing steed she spied a fiery trail snaking toward the scaffold. Gray powder was guiding the flame toward a keg lashed to a corner pillar. Her eyes widened. Unless Dudley retreated, they all would be blown to the clouds.

In the trampled snow she spied her grandfather's knife. She seized the weapon and jumped to her feet. Taking quick aim, she slung the blade into the animal's rump. The stallion squealed and bounded down the road, carrying Dudley with him.

"Well done, lass," Grandfather said. "Come along."

He grabbed her arm and urged her toward the shore. At the water's edge he threw her to the ground and flung himself on top of her. A fiery blast shattered the scaffold. Tremors shook the earth and fragments of black wood hurtled skyward. Hot wind singed the ground. Ash was settling over the snow as Grandfather raised his head. The gallows was a splintered carcass.

"Well," he said, wiping soot from his sleeves, "they shan't be dangling anyone on that gibbet for a while."

"Rachel," came a voice from the mist. "Are you all right?"

"Father," she said, rising to embrace the ghoul approaching her.

"We've precious little time for pleasantries," Grandfather said. "They'll be back soon enough. Man the boat, both of you."

Winslow bundled Rachel into the skiff and seated himself at a pair of oars near the bow. Grandfather shoved off and splashed into the stern.

"Handsomely with your rowing, lad," the old man said. "Rachel, take the tiller. Steer us into the harbor."

He grabbed a second pair of sweeps and bent his back to them.

"Heave, man, heave," he said. "Give it all you've got. We'll not be safe until the fog covers us."

Twenty-four

An Empty Nest

"Fools," Dudley bellowed at his soldiers. "To the water's edge."

The explosion had knocked away his tricornered hat and skewed his wig. His scarlet coat and white breeches were blackened by ash. With great difficulty he mastered his terrified mount and goaded the animal back to the shore. As the stallion splashed through the shallows, Dudley watched the skiff bounce across the choppy waters. Two masked phantoms tugged at the oars, and Rachel Winslow gripped the tiller.

"Imbeciles," Dudley shouted at his men. "Form up. Prime your weapons and reload."

The soldiers lined shoulder to shoulder. From their leather pouches they extracted paper cartridges and tore them open with their teeth. Black powder was sprinkled into each flash pan, and the sparking plates snapped shut. Charges were poured into muzzles, followed by ball and wadding.

"Hurry, you dogs," Dudley said. "Draw your rammers and ram down your cartridges."

He swatted the men with the flat of his sword while their ramrods pumped up and down. A veil of fog enveloped the skiff. Dudley marked the spot.

"Cock your firelocks," he said. The soldiers clicked back their flint hammers.

"Present arms. Take aim along my direction."

He stretched his arm over the waves.

"Make ready, and fire."

Shots boomed across the water. Dudley listened for a sharp cry, but heard none. He watched for the boat to wallow back into view. It did not.

"Confounded fog," he said. "You men, come with me."

He spurred his mount back to the gate. With his sword hilt he pounded on the timbers.

"Open," he shouted. "Open, I say, in the name of the king."

"Who goes there?"

"Idiot. I am Capt. Dudley, of his majesty's 64th. Open this gate at once."

Chains clattered. The gate swung back, and Dudley squeezed through the gap.

Before him milled a silent mob of citizens and blackened Indians. Scarlet ranks surrounded them, and beyond the crimson ring bristled a thicket of rifle muzzles. In the space separating them stood a young lieutenant addressing the night watchman.

"Good friend," the lieutenant said, "we wish no harm to any among you. Disperse, I pray you, and no charges will be pressed."

"We've no grievance against you or your men," said the watchman, "but we cannot fall back without assurance that Rachel Winslow is unharmed."

Dudley advanced his horse to the lieutenant's side.

"What in heaven's name are you about?" he said.

"Parley, my lord," the lieutenant said, trying not to notice Dudley's disheveled uniform.

"You are bargaining with those ruffians?"

"My lord, they surround us. If we fire upon them, they will kill us by the dozen."

"You are soldiers of the king. They are a rabble. Do your duty."

"What is our duty, my lord? To start a slaughter among kinsmen?"

"They are pig's whelps," Dudley said. "You desecrate the king's uniform by bartering with them."

"They are well hidden, as my lord can plainly see. We are ill-deployed to meet them. I think a confrontation under these conditions most unwise."

"They are spineless jellyfish," Dudley said, "a formation of farmers. Fire a volley into their midst and watch them flee. Do so at once, Lieutenant. I must get through."

The lieutenant glared at Dudley.

"If my lord wishes to start a war," he said, "let him be the one to issue the order. But my lord must be sure of this: for every two we kill of them, they will kill twelve of us."

"Insolent coward," Dudley said. "I'll have your neck in a noose for that. Company, make ready."

"My lord," the lieutenant said, "they ask only a fair trial for the prisoner, according to English law."

"A fair trial?" Dudley said. "Well, she shan't have it, because she's gone—escaped. Do you hear me, you sow's whelps? The lass has escaped. Now stand aside and let me pass."

A cheer erupted among the militia. The lieutenant groaned his relief. Citizens and Sons of Liberty echoed the militia's hurrahs.

"Boston militia, stand down," the watchman said.

"Troop, rest your firelocks," shouted the lieutenant. "We'll shed no English blood this day. Shoulder arms, and sound retreat."

Drummers beat the signal to withdraw. Already the min-utemen were shuffling in groups toward the town. Sons of Liberty began slipping through the lines of soldiers.

"Lieutenant," Dudley said. "I need your swiftest soldiers. We may yet catch the wench."

"If it please my lord . . ."

"Immediately," Dudley said. "You men, form up behind me. This way, quick march."

He forced his mount through the mob, and the soldiers pressed after him. Precious seconds were slipping away.

"Hurry on, you louts," he said, beating the soldiers with his crop. "Follow me, quick march."

He spurred his horse forward, fuming. What sort of fool did this peasant girl take him for? He knew exactly where she would go, and he would easily intercept her there. Through the streets and squares he raced, cursing the soldiers' sloth and goading them on with his crop. At last they approached the Winslow house.

"Surround it," Dudley said. "Let no one escape. You four, follow me."

He urged his mount onto the porch. The animal kicked in the door, and Dudley squeezed his steed through the opening. Horse and rider filled the front hall, where Dudley tangled his wig in the chandelier. He freed the hairpiece and leapt from his saddle.

The parlor was empty—not merely empty, but denuded. Not a stick of furniture populated the chamber. Pictures had been stripped from the walls, and the Brussels carpet was missing from the floor. He yanked free his sword and rushed into the dining room. It, too, was vacant.

"Hallo," he said. "Who's there?"

No one answered.

With mounting fury he dashed from room to room, his boots echoing on bare walls. He climbed the stairs and searched the upper rooms, finding only stray cobwebs.

"Blast," he shouted, punching his sword hilt through a window pane.

After a moment's thought he descended the stairs and seized his horse's reins. Back outside he dragged the animal.

"Form up," he shouted, swinging into his saddle. "Follow me to the harbor."

Twenty-five

❦

The Schooner

Rachel braced the skiff's tiller under her arm and steered for the gray harbor waters.

"Pull, man, pull," Grandfather urged Winslow. The two men heaved at the oars, ramming the boat through the choppy waves.

"Rachel, make ready to alter course," Grandfather said, "on my command."

Veils of fog were already masking the shore.

"Steady, lass," Grandfather said, "steady as she goes. Keep your head forward and mind me."

Rachel's throat was parched, and her hands trembled on the tiller. Any moment she expected a bullet in the back. With hawk's eyes Grandfather concentrated on the shore.

"Steady," he said, "steady . . . a few more seconds and . . . now, lass, hard a'starboard."

She jerked the tiller to her chest. With her feet shoved beneath a plank she leaned as far over the stern as she dared. Water splashed the back of her head. The boat pitched and rolled toward Dorchester Flats.

"Well done, lass," Grandfather said. "Bring her amidships and hold your course. Quick, child. Aye, that's it. Now, Winslow, pull for all you're worth."

The men groaned as they tugged on the sweeps. Rachel peered ashore and saw only gray mist. A volley of shots rang out. The musket balls splashed astern.

"Hah," Grandfather said. "Poor shooting, that. Steady as she goes, Rachel. Them redcoats may take a second shot at us. Fifty yards more, and we'll steer to port again."

"Where are we bound?" she said.

"The *Annalee* is waiting in the harbor," Winslow said between pulls. "She's the fastest ship I've got. Your mother's already aboard. With the Lord's blessing we'll be past the headlands before the fog lifts. Goodness, child, this mask is uncomfortable. How did you bear it?"

"Mine became a second skin to me," she said.

"I prefer your first skin. Much prettier."

Minutes passed without a second volley.

"They've flown the roost," Grandfather said. "Heading back into Boston, most likely. A'fore long there'll be soldiers on every wharf watching for us. Rachel, steer her back to port. Keep your eyes sharp for the *Annalee*."

The men eased their rowing. Grandfather tugged off his mask and began whistling a whippoorwill's cry into the mist. Before long the call returned to him.

"A bit more to port, child," Winslow said. Grandfather continued to whistle, and each reply drew nearer. At last a dark hull loomed off the bow.

"I see her," Rachel said.

"Bring us alongside," Grandfather said, "easy now."

She steered toward the schooner. The *Annalee* was a sleek vessel built for speed, with a razor bow and graceful lines. Her two masts climbed at a rakish angle into the fog. As the skiff brushed the ship's side, Winslow tossed a mooring line to waiting crewmen. Rachel was soon climbing the chains to the ship's waist.

"Darling," her mother said, embracing her. "Thank God you're well. We heard shots."

"They missed," Rachel said. "We are all unhurt."

"Not quite," Grandfather said as he hauled himself over the rail. "We're still in the lion's maw, every blessed one of us. You lasses get yourselves below, and let us pry ourselves loose."

"Deck, there," Winslow said, swinging aboard. "Man the winches. Weigh anchor. You lads, prepare to set jibs and foresail. Sullivan, get your leads forward and begin soundings. Pomeroy, man the helm."

"Aye, sir," came a chorus of replies. Barefooted crewmen padded in all directions.

"Come below, Rachel," Mrs. Winslow said.

"No, Mother, I'll stay topside. How did you know of my trouble?"

"Your grandfather, God bless him. He did a bit of ghost-ing himself and learned you were to be taken to the Neck at dawn."

"Then you must also know that I was Regina Silsby."

"Again, 'twas your grandfather," Mrs. Winslow said. "He's been traipsing after you almost from the first."

"No," Rachel said. "Do you mean to say that he knew all along?"

"I could scarcely believe the adventures he told us. Re-ally, Rachel. You are as audacious as . . . well, as your grand-father was at your age. I must say he has certainly enjoyed himself, following you about and watching you work. He contrived this little rescue, while your father scraped together every crewman in his employ. We spent all night packing the house, and by dawn everything was stowed aboard ship."

"Everything, Mother? Do you mean . . . ?"

"The entire house is empty," Mrs. Winslow said. "Capt. Dudley will have quite a shock when he comes looking for his next meal. Your father had the *Annalee* moved to Boston Neck to retrieve you, while the other ships set sail for the open sea. They should be past the headlands by now."

"Rachel," Winslow said, "take your mother below."

"Please, Father, we wish to stay on deck."

"Very well, then. To the taffrail with the both of you, and stay out of the way. By heaven, I may not know how to haunt a town or blast a gallows, but I can well enough sail a ship."

"Anchor's up short," came a cry from the bow.

"Haul her up and make her fast," Winslow said. "Hoist the jibs and loose the foresail battens. Ready on the braces."

Two triangular sails flapped open over the bowsprit. The ship veered away from the wind.

"Up the foresail," Winslow said. "Belay those jib sheets. Pomeroy, set a course east nor'east. We'll slide right under the south shore."

The sails stiffened, and the schooner plied forward.

"All hands," Winslow said. "Every one of you knows what my daughter's been up to these past weeks."

"Hear, hear. Well done, Rachel. There's a stout lass."

"We're beating up the harbor channel toward the head-lands," Winslow said. "We've a town full of angry soldiers to port and a hundred British warships to starboard. Every man among us has got to keep quiet. Not a sound—understood?"

The crew nodded. Winslow lowered his tone and said, "Leadsman, what's the soundings?"

"Deep water, Captain. We're in the channel."

"Well done. Helm, hold your course."

Grandfather paced to Winslow's side.

"Fog's lifting," the old man murmured.

"Aye," Winslow agreed. "Confound it all. Even if we escape the harbor fleet, those guns on the South Battery will pulverize us."

"Twenty-four pounders," Grandfather said. "They'll make flotsam of us in short order. And we've still got Castle Island to contend with."

Winslow stretched open a spyglass and directed it toward the town.

"Can't see a thing," he said. "We've only a cable's length between the wharves and the harbor ships. If we sail too fast, we could run afoul of one or the other."

Grandfather nodded. Winslow snapped shut the glass and said, "I suppose we'll have to chance it. Ho, men. Hoist the mainsail, quietly as you can. Unfurl the staysails and topsails. You, there. Man the braces, and ready on the sheets. Benson, get yourself to the jib boom and give warning if you see anything dead ahead. Helm, stand ready to alter course."

"Aye, sir."

The schooner was soon heeling to port under a full spread of sail.

"Wind's strengthening," Winslow said, noting the hum in the rigging. "It'll blow off the fog quick enough. I put our speed at eight knots."

"Maybe nine," Grandfather said. "Can't say I ever sailed through Boston harbor this swiftly. Downright reckless."

"Are you complaining?"

"Complimenting."

To starboard loomed a shadowy warship. Shouted orders drifted from the towering wooden walls, accompanied by a scrape of holystone scrubbing the decks. Yardarms and shrouds were frosted with ice. The vessel drifted astern and vanished into the fog.

"Listen," Grandfather said, nodding to port. Winslow perked his ears and detected a steady clatter ashore.

"Shopkeepers along the quays," he said.

"Griffin's Wharf, I'll wager," Grandfather said. "We're about one hundred fifty yards offshore."

"Helm, bring us a point closer to the wind," Winslow said. "Deck there. Tighten up on those sheets. Mind your luffing."

He tugged open his telescope and squinted once more through the lens.

"Blind as a bat," he said, collapsing the glass again. "We'll have to gauge when we round the South Battery. Rachel, you've a good set of ears. Make yourself useful and see if you can hear the soldiers drilling at Fort Hill."

She eased across the sloping deck to her father's side. Gripping a main stay, she leaned over the rail and cocked an ear toward shore. Gray waves and white foam rolled past her shoulders as she listened intently to the sounds drifting over the water. Through the fog came a distant clopping of horses and rumbling of wagons. Hammers tapped and voices chattered. Somewhere a handbell clanged and a drum rapped.

"Hah," she said, stabbing a finger into the mist. "The King's Chapel is chiming. And there to the north I hear Christ Church."

"Quarter to seven," Winslow said, glancing at his watch. "That puts the battery off the port bow. At seven sharp we should be ready for a tack to starboard. Leadsman, keep reporting your soundings. We'll be closing on Noddles Island a'fore long. Rachel, steady with your listening, and point out for me the South Battery, when you can. There's a good girl."

She remained at her post, clutching the stays as the wind tousled her skirts and hair, her ears fixed on the cacophony ashore. The town's clatter faded into emptiness, leaving only the wash of the waves. Back and forth her father paced the quarter deck, constantly studying his timepiece and stretching his telescope toward shore. Grandfather roamed the midships eyeing every sail and ordering adjustments to sheets and stays. Her mother stood at the taffrail, her lips moving in silent prayer.

Isolated flakes of snow began to brush the sails. The tiny crystals soon thickened into tumbling sheets.

"Mr. Benson," Winslow said. "Send a couple hands aloft to keep those gaffs and sails swept down. Don't let any ice form on the canvas."

"Aye, sir."

"Father," Rachel said. "The King's Chapel is chiming seven o'clock."

She pointed off the port quarter.

"I hear it," Winslow said, "and not a moment too soon. Leadsman, what's our depth?"

"Five fathoms, Captain. We've just crossed the center of the sea channel."

"All hands, ready about. Helm, prepare to make course south east, on my command."

"Aye, Captain."

Winslow stared toward the invisible town, counting the seconds to himself.

"Four-and-a-half fathoms," the leadsman said.

All eyes turned to Rachel's father. His gaze was fixed astern, his fingers nervously drumming his closed telescope.

"Four fathoms, Captain. Noddle's Island's dead ahead."

"Steady as she goes," Winslow said.

"Three-and-a-half fathoms, Captain. Shoaling fast. Three fathoms."

"Release the braces," Winslow said. "Loose the sheets. Helm, hard a lee."

The schooner lurched into the wind. Sails flapped violently, shedding ice. For several moments the *Annalee* wallowed in the waves. Suddenly she leaned to starboard. Fore and main booms swung across the deck and banged to a stop over the starboard rail. Canvas stiffened, and the ship surged forward.

"Belay sheets," Winslow said. "Fix the braces."

"Helm's south east, Captain."

"Hold your course."

"Look there," Grandfather said, pointing forward. The snowfall abruptly ceased. Beyond the bowsprit stretched an open sea channel under a leaden sky. Clouds and swirling snow were retreating across the islands that fringed the waterway.

"Helm, hold her steady to the port side of the channel," Winslow said. "With the Lord's favor we'll clear Castle Island before the fog rolls off her."

"Aye, sir."

Winslow turned his attention astern. Church spires pierced the haze that smothered the town, and Beacon Hill bulged like a slumbering granite beast beyond.

"Magnificent," Rachel said.

"Mark it well," he told her. " 'Twill be the last time you gaze upon Boston for a long while."

A lump lodged in her throat. The only home she had ever known was rapidly vanishing astern. Months, or even years, might pass before she beheld again the house in which she was born.

"Father," she said, remembering her brother, "what's to become of Robert?"

"I sent some lads searching for him," Winslow said, "but he was nowhere to be found. We'll have to send word to him after we're away."

"Faneuil Hall rooftop's visible," Grandfather said, pointing astern, "and there's the State House."

"We'll be seeing the South Battery before long," Winslow said, "and they'll be seeing us. Leadsman, what's our sounding?"

"Four fathoms, Captain."

"Helm, hold your course. Don't let us drift too much to leeward. We can't afford to tack in the channel."

"Aye, Captain."

"Three thousand yards from the battery," Winslow guessed, squinting through his telescope. "We're still in range of those guns."

"They can't see us yet," Grandfather said. " 'Tis a pretty piece of navigating so far, I'd say."

Winslow mopped his brow. Governor's Island slid by the port rail. Beyond the starboard bow rose the tiny bluff of Castle Island. A granite fortress flying the Union Jack crowned the peak. Mrs. Winslow waved her kerchief at the sentries pacing the walls. The soldiers returned her greeting.

"Father," Rachel said, "may I have your spyglass?"

"Certainly, dearest," he said, passing it to her. She climbed the rail by the main stays and stretched the telescope toward Boston.

"I can barely make out the end of Long Wharf," she said, her skirts billowing about her. "Why, bless my soul."

"What is it, child?"

"I do believe I see Capt. Dudley," she said. "Aye, it must be so. He's on horseback at the tip of the pier, with soldiers all about him. His uniform's all blackened by the gallows explosion. He's bouncing up and down in his saddle and waving his arms and pointing this way."

"He's seen us," Winslow said.

"Now he's galloping ashore. No, wait. He's coming back and dismounting. He's drubbing a soldier, and *that* fellow is mounting and galloping ashore."

"Bound for the South Battery," Winslow said.

" 'Twill be four minutes a'fore he arrives," Grandfather said. "Two to report and another three to train the guns. We may be out of range by then."

"Of the South Battery, aye," Winslow said. "But Castle Island?"

"That's another matter," Grandfather said. "They'll load up and run out at the first shot from the shore."

"Dudley's climbing into a boat," Rachel said. "The soldiers are following after him. Whoops! Dear me, one has fallen into the water. Not to worry, he's swimming ashore. Dudley's ignoring him. They're rowing into the harbor. What a tangled mess. Those soldiers are making for bad seamen. The boat's rocking about and the oars are flailing everywhere. Now I've lost them in the fog."

"Heading for the fleet," Winslow said. "If any of those ships should give chase . . ."

He peered aloft and studied the sails.

"We may yet squeeze another quarter-knot out of her," he said.

"Deck, there. Run out the flying jib boom and haul up the storm jibs on her. Rig the spanker abaft the mainsail. Handsomely, now."

The added canvas was soon stiffening fore and aft, and the schooner barreled through the sea lane. Spray showered her bows and cascaded along the deck.

"I see signal flags on the South Battery," Rachel said.

"Give me that," Grandfather said, taking the glass from her. "Let me see. They're ordering a general chase. By my faith, that maniac is sending the entire fleet after us."

"Can he do that?" Rachel said. "He's but a captain of infantry."

"He's also an earl's son," Grandfather said. "The fleet's not answering, but they can't see the signal yet for the fog. Castle Island's still under the weather, so they're blind to it as well. I expect the fleet'll wake up when Capt. Dudley's boat hails them. Most likely he'll argue with the officer on deck and get a cutter or two, perhaps a frigate."

"Trouble for us," Winslow said.

"We've a good start on them," Grandfather said. "*Annalee's* faster than anything the redcoats have afloat, and she can sail a few points closer to the wind. They'll have to tack down the channel."

"Who's that making sail?" Rachel said. Grandfather peered through the scope at a pair of canvas sheets swelling above the fog.

" 'Tis a sixty-four gunner, by the look of her," he said. "The *Romney*, I'll wager. By my faith, that Dudley's got more clout than I credited him for. Looks like a frigate making sail as well."

"They'll be a thousand yards closer to us than the shore guns," Winslow said.

A cannon boomed. Smoke plumed from the wall of the South Battery. The shot whizzed overhead and splashed twenty yards beyond the bow.

"Gauging the range," Grandfather said.

A second gun thundered. That ball, too, whistled overhead and splashed into the waves.

"Helm," Winslow said, "on my command, fall off a point from the wind."

"Aye, sir."

Winslow turned to Grandfather and said, "Perhaps we can make them miss."

"Worth a try," the old man agreed. "There's a bustle brewing on Castle Island."

Scores of soldiers were scampering along the fortress walls. A dozen telescopes trained on the schooner.

Winslow returned his gaze astern and spied a telltale puff of white smoke rise from the south battery.

"Helm, fall off a point," he said. "Loose the sheets and . . . hold there. Belay."

Annalee eased to starboard. Seconds passed. The gun's thunder finally reached the schooner, followed by a whistling shot that threw up a geyser to port.

"Chain shot," Grandfather said. "They'll try to cripple our masts and slow us down."

"Helm, bring her up two points," Winslow said.

"Two points, aye."

"Close haul sheets and belay."

Annalee clawed toward the wind, leaping the waves and shooting clouds of spray. Winslow continued to concentrate on the battery. Two puffs plumed together.

"Helm, fall off a point," Winslow said. "Loose sheets and belay."

Both shots fell astern. Another ball dropped even farther behind.

"We've outrun them," Grandfather said.

"Well done," Winslow said. "Helm, bring her up a point. Steady as she goes."

"Steady as she goes, aye."

"Father, look," Rachel said. From the harbor fog emerged a massive warship, her fore and main topsails easing her into the sea channel. The great hull blotted out the South Battery just as the yardarms dropped, spilling the wind from their sails. Already the ship's starboard gun ports were opening. Her wooden wall became a checkerboard of dark holes separated by varnished oak. Anchors splashed at the bow and stern, holding the ship in the mouth of the channel. A graceful frigate slid behind the warship and stationed herself off the man-o'-war's bow. Both had signal flags fluttering from their yardarms.

"Deck, there," Winslow shouted. "Take that luff out of that foresail."

"*Romney's* signaling Castle Island," Grandfather said, studying the flags through the spyglass. "They're telling the fort we've got Regina Silsby aboard."

"That castle will pulverize us," Winslow said. "We've nothing but open channel ahead."

"Three miles of clear shooting," Grandfather said.

The two men exchanged a rueful glance.

"What now?" Winslow said.

"A warning shot across our bow," Grandfather said, "and we'll have to heave to. Otherwise . . ."

Winslow nodded. With slumped shoulders he approached his daughter.

"Rachel, come here, child," he said, and put his arm around her. "I'm afraid they've got us in a pickle barrel. We can't escape the Castle Island guns."

She pondered the implications. *Annalee* would be forced to back her sails and wait for the frigate to bear down on her. Her father and grandfather would be jailed, probably hanged, and every crewman aboard the schooner pressed into service for the Royal Navy. Rachel herself might find a noose about her neck, leaving her mother to suffer a desolate widowhood.

"Oh, Father," she said, burying her face in his breast. "What have I done to you?"

" 'Twasn't you who's done it, dear," he said, kissing her brow. "I've brought it upon myself."

"Can you ever forgive me?"

"Come, come, lass. Chin up. We've made a good run of it and should be proud of that. Whatever's in store we'll face bravely, like men, shan't we?"

"Aye," she said, wiping her eyes and managing a smile, "like men."

"Castle Island's acknowledging the *Romney's* signal," Grandfather said, his glass trained on the fortress. "Wait, what's this?"

He toweled the spyglass lens with his shirt tail and pressed it to his eye again.

"Bless my soul," he said.

"What?" Winslow said.

"Castle Island's calling off the action," Grandfather said, "by order of the acting governor."

"You don't say."

"I do say. All forces are commanded positively not to fire on us. The ships are acknowledging. You hear that, lads? Col. Leslie's called a halt to it. We're free and clear."

The crew shouted hurrahs. Rachel threw her arms about her father's neck and squealed her glee. With his spyglass Grandfather was already inspecting the fortress.

"Why, look there, Rachel," he said. "On the east rampart of the castle—'tis your Col. Leslie, I believe."

Rachel accepted the glass and scanned the fortress. Standing in his shirt sleeves atop the eastern wall was the hatless Col. Leslie. Stiff breezes were teasing the unknotted lace at his throat. A scowl curled his lips as he trained his telescope on the *Annalee*. For a moment he and Rachel eyed each other through their extended lenses. Slowly she lowered her glass, flashed the colonel a grateful smile, and blew him a kiss. Leslie dropped his telescope and returned her salutation with a wave. He then wheeled about and disappeared from view.

Already the *Romney's* gun ports were closing. A pair of long boats descended the ship's side, preparing to guide her back to her mooring. Similar boats slid from the rails of the frigate.

Mrs. Winslow stood at the *Annalee's* stern rail, watching the retreating ships.

"Thank You, gracious Lord," she said.

Twenty-six

Liberty

"Rachel," Grandfather said from the *Annalee's* stern rail. "You may want to see this."

He handed her the spyglass.

"On the *Romney's* quarterdeck," he said. "Your precious Capt. Dudley is making a spectacle of himself."

"Why, bless my soul," she said, peering through the lens. "He does seem frustrated, doesn't he?"

"Bit of a tantrum he's throwing, I'd say."

"One officer's been shoved on his rump," she said. "Goodness me, there goes another. Dudley's jumping up and down and waving his arms and pointing our way. Now the ship's captain is signaling his Royal Marines. They're surrounding

Dudley. They've taken his sword and pinned his arms behind his back. How rude. The future Earl of Leicester is being carried below decks."

"To the brig, I expect," Grandfather said. "It appears that a glorious military career is coming to a most ignoble end."

"Serves him right," Mrs. Winslow said. "Try to kill my daughter, will he?"

With the telescope Rachel made a final inspection of Castle Island.

"There's Col. Leslie again," she said, "on the ramparts with a spyglass directed at the *Romney*. He must be watching Dudley's spectacle too. And he is smiling. Fancy that."

"Perhaps the colonel shares our opinion of the future earl," Grandfather said. "Ho, lass, watch your pockets there. You're about to lose something."

Rachel thrust a hand into her skirt and discovered Regina Silsby's manuscript working itself loose.

"What is it you've got there?" he said. "You look ready to cut off someone's fingers over it."

The truth could not be avoided. Rachel squared her shoulders and said, "It is Regina Silsby's final piece, given me by Mr. Newcomb. I intend to keep it in honor of my great-aunt."

"Do you, now?" he said. "Very well, if you feel so strongly about it. I suppose you'll be wanting the rest of her works also."

"Grandfather, do you know where they are?"

"Safe and sound in my sea chest, where they've been these last thirty years. High time we heard them again."

"Oh, Grandfather," she said, embracing him. "You didn't burn them."

"Mercy's sake, child. Why would I do a thing like that?"

"Did you not think her a witch?"

"I thought nothing of the sort. I said she was best left alone. 'Twas meant as a warning for you, to stop your tomfoolery while you still had a head on your shoulders."

"Rachel," Winslow said. "What say you change your clothes and man the helm there? We'll be sailing due south after we pass the capes."

"Where are we bound, Father?"

"Philadelphia. You've cousins there, you know. Can't wait to see the looks on their faces when we arrive at their doorstep. Come to think of it, they might find your adventures most entertaining."

"Belay that thought," Grandfather said. " 'Twould be better not to share a word with anyone. 'Tis an unsavory reputation we've left behind in Boston, and Col. Leslie won't be acting governor forever. Them redcoats may well descend on us by the hundred. We'd have to flee farther south."

"To Virginia, perhaps?" Rachel said. "Or the Carolinas? There's good sailing to be had there."

"And warmer climes," her mother said. "I do tire of these northern winters."

"Please," Winslow said, "let us first try our fortunes in Philadelphia. We've family there and can set up a good business in short order. Now, Rachel, promise me there'll be no running about Philadelphia as Regina Silsby's ghost. If you keep that up, we shall quickly run out of havens."

"Mercy, Father," she said. "I doubt very much that Regina Silsby will find any mischief to make in Philadelphia."

Author's Note

By his prudent action, Colonel Leslie postponed
war in America for one year. In April of 1775, the
new military governor of Massachusetts ordered
rebel stores of gunpowder seized at Lexington and
Concord. Local militias, alerted by Paul Revere and
William Dawes, gathered on the towns' commons
to oppose the British forces. Shots were exchanged,
igniting the American Revolution.